Newcastle
Short Story Award

HUNTER
WRITERS
CENTRE

First published in Australia in 2024 by Hunter Writers' Centre
www.hunterwriterscentre.org
Newcastle Short Story Award 2023
ISBN 978-0-6453756-5-7

Edited by
Winnie Dunn

Cover photograph by
Sarah Gentle

Published by Hunter Writers' Centre Inc. 2024

The 2023 Newcastle Short Story Award Anthology is produced
primarily on Awabakal country, from work created on
this and other Aboriginal and Torres Strait Islander lands.

Hunter Writers' Centre
Newcastle NSW 2300

hunterwriterscentre.org

Judges' report

Angela Meyer and Winnie Dunn

Judging the 2023 Newcastle Short Story Award was a pleasure. The entries delighted, moved, surprised, and entertained us. The high-quality submissions featured compelling stories with strong voices, well-rounded characters, promising setups, and fulfilling endings.

The shortlisted stories exhibit diverse perspectives, settings, tones, and character journeys. They stand out for their craftsmanship, subtlety, coherence, and the skilful weaving of narrative threads by the authors. Congratulations to the shortlisted authors—enjoy their works in this anthology!

The winner of this year's Newcastle Short Story Award is an exceptional piece of literary fiction by a promising emerging writer. 'Kuya' follows the story of a queer Filipino-Australian boy from Western Sydney who is forced to recognise the intricacies of not only his sexuality and culture, but the complex inner-worlds of his disabled brother and neurotic mother. This is a feat skilfully navigated with tight structure, clear plot, original sentences, and memorable characters. With nuance and compassion, 'Kuya' reveals to readers an integral and intersectional part of Australia—all with an expert touch of humour.

Coming in at second place, with the strongest and most unique dialogue of the bunch, is 'Papamosque,' a thrilling short story of youth, crime, bigotry, and class. The characters and plot are raw and unkempt, yet wide-eyed with childhood naivety—allowing readers to sympathise with the harsher aspects of Australian culture that are all-too-often swept under the rug. This is a captivating piece of fiction from an exciting talent.

In third place, 'Tadpole' is a unique and tender coming-of-age tale. Nature and childhood are interwoven with well-written imagery that makes the harsh contrasts of prey/predator, native/invasive, parent/child, and life/death gentler yet more immediate. A climate change allegory is very rarely told from such purposeful duality. 'Tadpole' is a melancholic read, in the best way possible.

We highly commended two stories. The messiness of meet-cutes, dating apps, and sexuality is revealed with utter delight in 'First Impressions.' The narrator is sassy, foul-mouthed, and striving for clarity and independence—all at the phenomenal age of thirty-five! 'Lowanna's Fever,' meanwhile, returns the reader to original traditions of literature. Weaving colloquial vernacular, well thought-out characters, and culturally informed imagery, 'Lowanna's Fever' is a haunting, yet humorous, invocation of oral and historical storytelling—a stunning short story.

Three stories by Hunter region writers were awarded local awards. Packed with stunning sensory detail, 'It Begins' tells a poignant story of belonging and place, of the difficulties of staying, and leaving, home in the face of environmental threats. 'Mojo' similarly details, with great specificity, the build of dissatisfactions that lead to a life change, this time from cold to sunshine. 'The Calling' is entertaining and memorable, placing the reader in time with its use of vernacular, brand names, and a rollicking plot about a surfboard and a dodgy Carpet King.

The shortlisted stories are striking for their diversity and rich sense of culture and place. They offer fresh and thought-provoking perspectives on challenging contemporary issues, voicing experiences of loss and trauma, connection and disconnection, and the unease of living in a world marked by the material and psychological effects of climate change. This collection explores the edges of sexuality, family, and the intersectional complexities of multicultural Australia, asking poignant and powerful questions about identity, desire, and belonging.

We hope you are as moved, transported, inspired, and entertained as we were as you read through this anthology. As a book, it is a fascinating representation of a moment in time, and reflects much about coastal and regional Australia, and the concerns of people living in the area.

Happy reading,
Angela Meyer and Winnie Dunn

1st Prize donated by The University of Newcastle
Kuya — Patrick Cruz Forrest

2nd Prize donated by The University of Newcastle
Papamosque — Natalie A. Vella

3rd Prize donated by The University of Newcastle
Tadpole — Emma Bjorndahl

Highly Commended donated by FogHorn Brewhouse
First Impressions — Jessie Lambert
Lowanna's Fever — Adam Brannigan

Local Award donated by Macquariedale Organic Wines
It Begins — Grace Buckley

Local Award donated by Tulloch Wines
The Calling — Kate O'Connor

Local Award donated by Pepper Tree Wines
Mojo — Ingrid Woodrow

Contents

Kuya

Patrick Cruz Forrest

1st Prize

The sweaty underside of my thighs stuck to the banig. Its woven pattern left an imprint on my skin. Felix's hot, clammy, and twitching thigh kept brushing mine.

'Stooooop!' I said, pushing his knee away. He was too focused on the TV to pay me any attention.

Blonde hair up in loose mermaid waves pinned back to the sides, Lizzie McGuire shut a door while her best friend, Miranda, whispered something secret. I didn't know what Miranda said though because no sound was coming out of her mouth.

'Ma, Felix is making me watch on mute again!' I cried out.

'Ay naku Raymond,' Ma yelled from the kitchen. 'You'b seen dat show a millyon times alredy.'

Suddenly, a tune played: Do-do do-do do-do-do.

Felix threw his hands over his ears and started moaning. Elbows in the air, bone poking through skin. My brother Felix hated the doorbell song. I hated it too since it had the same melody as our school bell, which always led to the other boys calling me "Raymonda" for the next half an hour of recess, until it rang again.

That time however, it signalled something different. My tummy turned in tight knots, my balls shrunk up into my body, and my heart started beating so hard it climbed up my throat. I swallowed it all back down. *David is here.*

Slippers snapping against tile, Ma came running into the living room. A fishy smell followed her, making my nose scrunch up. Sweat patches seeped out from under her armpits onto her white singlet. Her thin black hair stuck up behind her head like a chicken tail and was held in place with a see-through brown claw clip that looked like a giant cockroach.

'Just a minit, Dabid!'

Ma barged through our bedroom door and tossed up into the air all the clothes that had been lying on our bed. A minute later, she came back out in a polo shirt with a deep V-neck collar, shutting the door behind her. Checking herself out in the mirror on the wall, Ma looked down at the line between her squished-up boobs and went to button her collar. But there were no buttons. This was because Felix had an annoying habit of tearing the buttons off all our clothes. Instead, Ma pulled the cockroach off the top of her head and used that. I thought it was embarrassing and I wanted to tell her to go back and change again. Felix meanwhile was bouncing on the banig to an ad for *Lilo & Stitch*.

The glow-in-the-dark rosary hanging on the doorknob swung to-and-fro as Ma opened the front door, giving mini plastic Jesus a good beating. David was standing against the dim 4pm sun. He was shaped like a giant slice of watermelon. Bowing his head, David stepped through the threshold, briefcase in hand—his hand was as hairy as a rambutan. Ma only came up to the middle of David's chest. 'Ya cookin' me dinner are ya?' David said, sniffing. 'Shoulda told ya I don't eat fish.' His laughter filled up the entire house. I felt the vibrations of it tickling me.

Ma smiled and smoothed her shirt over her tummy. She looked down at the pointed, tan leather shoes on David's feet. 'Ip you don't mind?'

David stood blank-faced for a few seconds before replying, 'Oh … course.'

Nodding, Ma dashed to the kitchen. David dropped onto the white couch against the back wall, setting his briefcase down on the coffee table. All of Ma's cushions disappeared behind his body. David leant over his lap to untie his shoes and the shiny lanyard around his neck caught in the groove in his chest, between his pecs, making me shudder. The attached card read: 'David Moore, Speech Pathologist,' and it was written in a crayon speech bubble.

As he reached forward, the muscles on the back of David's arms stuck out in the shape of an apostrophe. Using both hands, he pulled off each of his shoes and unveiled two long feet. The black socks stretched thin enough to see the skin of his toes.

'Why're you watching this girl's show?' he asked me.

I wanted to say, 'It's not a girl's show!' but my mouth wouldn't cooperate. What I really wanted to say was, 'Can you flex your biceps?'

All I could manage was to point at Felix, who was sitting on the banig with his legs crossed, mouth open, face lit up purple and pink by the square TV. David laughed. Then he winked at me and I shrivelled up like a sultana.

***

TV static prickled my nose as I sat right in front of the screen to hear what Lizzie McGuire was saying to her mother. 'I want a bra!' she screamed. *A bra? Why does she need a bra for those itty bitties?*

I would've found out the answer if not for David. Just as Lizzie clutched her kickboard-flat chest, David's voice carried from the other side of the wall. 'Well, wot can Felix actually say?'

'Only us,' Ma's voice answered. 'He knows only how to call us.'

'Ya got a photo handy?'

'Anak, come here!'

I shot up and stepped into my slippers. My heels hung over the back edge of them, and the strap bit the skin between my toes.

The kitchen smelled exactly like the Chinese seafood shop outside the bus stop at Mount Druitt station, which always reminded me of sticking my head in a bin. *Poor David.* He probably wasn't used to smells like this.

He was sitting at the dining table with his back to me, collecting a bunch of laminated cards that spread out before him. His shirt stretched across the mountains of his shoulder blades. Each of the cards on the table had a Velcro label stuck to them. Felix was putting a label that read 'Spoon' onto a picture of a dog. I gawked as my brother tore the Velcro off and on, over and over again. As he pulled, Felix tilted his ear down towards the table and laughed at the tssshp sound.

Hot with embarrassment, Ma was fanning herself with a pamaypay that had a picture of Mary on it. Her straight mouth quickly bent into a smile when she noticed me. 'Anak, get da pamily pickchur ob us sa Batangas,' she said, pointing to the fridge with puckered lips.

I walked over to where the fridge, stove and pantry were lined up against the yellow tiles, separated with big sheets of cardboard from the boxes they came in. There was a pot rattling on the stove, like the hi-hats in *Crazy in Love.*

How can David work in a such a loud place like this?

The photo of us in Batangas was fixed to the fridge under a magnet shaped like a Jeepney. In it, Me, Ma, Felix, and Pa stood on a grey beach against a white and foamy ocean, flanked by some droopy palm trees. Felix was sleeping in his pram, all his limbs hanging out. Pa stood behind me with his shirt folded up, showing us all his beer belly. It was the most time we'd ever spent with him. I was wearing a singlet, my stick-like arms painted white with sunscreen so that they looked more like bare bones.

'Bilis, Anak!'

I jumped and ran the photo to the table. Ma pointed her lips towards David. I showed it to him and he snatched it from my grip. Holding my breath, I shuffled behind Ma and watched over her shoulder.

'Righto,' David said, sliding the photo under Felix. 'Who's this?'

Felix looked down at the photo, put a finger in his big ear and started moaning again, his face scrunched up like he just bit into a lemon. Ma shook her head and started massaging her withered temples. The pot continued to rattle on the stove.

'Come on, mate. Who's this fella?' David asked Felix again.

Felix cupped his right ear with his small, bony hand.

'Shhst! Makinig ka,' Ma hissed. 'You listen!'

With one hand over his ear, Felix used his other hand to point over Ma's shoulder to me. There was dirt beneath his nails. David looked up in my direction. I straightened my back.

'What's 'is name?' David asked Felix.

'Kuya Raymond,' Felix answered.

David jerked his head towards Ma, his mouth open as though Felix had said something naughty.

'Ku-we-ah?' he asked.

'Ay! No,' Ma shot back. 'Not queer,' she said through closed teeth. 'Kooh-yah. It means big brahder in Pilipino.'

David nodded slowly, the corner of his mouth twitching. I knew exactly what that look meant. It was the same look the boys at school gave me whenever I accidentally answered to Raymonda. It was the kind of look that made me feel like my organs were melting inside me.

'Righto. And this one?' David said, pointing to someone else in the photo.

'Mba Mba,' Felix replied.

'Papa,' Ma corrected, when David looked to her with his heavy brow raised.

I watched as David put his huge, sharp face right in front of Felix's. David enunciated, 'Pa-pa.'

Still, Felix responded with, 'Mbaba.'

With a groan of frustration, David put his rude finger and thumb over Felix's mouth, pressing my brother's lips together. The two were close enough to kiss. Felix opened his mouth and Ma's pot stopped rattling at the exact moment that David's finger slipped under Felix's top-lip.

The Sydney 2000 clock ticking on the wall over the microwave was the only reason I knew time hadn't really frozen.

Oh my gosh. Did Felix just suck on David's finger? I bet it tasted just like salt and vinegar chips.

Between my thighs, I got all warm and tingly. It felt kind of like I needed to wee but in a different way, in a sort of good way. We learned about this at school, but it wasn't supposed to happen now. Not like this. I touched my shaking knees together, tried to squeeze the feeling out. It only made it stronger.

I curled over and glared at my younger brother. *It's so unfair! Felix always gets what he wants!*

He got to have the TV on mute whenever he was in the room, even if the whole family was watching. He got to play with Barbies and Bratz and nobody ever said anything to him about dolls only being for girls. And now he got to have David.

'Papa!' Felix and David were repeating together. Ma was clapping, her shoulders bouncing with laughter. It was the first time Felix had ever made a 'P' sound. Ma reached behind her to grab my hand, but I stepped back out of her reach. The kitchen was so hot and it smelt so bad. It made me sick.

'Ano bayan, Raymond?'

Shaking my head, I ran down the hall, my body bent like a crooked nail to hide my shame.

'Crikey. What's up with Queer Raymond?' I heard David ask behind me.

12

Papamosque

Natalie A. Vella

2nd Prize

In the drain outlet I saw a gun surrounded by discarded nappies and garbage. My brother, Jabba, was up ahead running the front tyre of his Kmart version of a BMX over a trail of ants. I grabbed the gun before he could lay his hands on it. It was heavy. Cold. So big it swallowed my small hands and pulled down my arm with the weight of it. I turned the gun over, running my fingers over the metal grooves. The smooth muzzle was slim.

I pointed the barrel at Jabba, resting my finger on the trigger. 'Hands up.'

His black eye, which had turned a custard yellow colour, glared at me. 'Is that fake?'

'Nah, I reckon it's real.'

'Bullshit.'

He wanted to hold it. I could tell by the way his bottom lip jutted out. He always wanted what I wanted. Jabba ran towards me. 'Can I look? It must belong to the gunman on the news.'

I turned around and pointed the gun at the concrete wall of the creek bed. 'Dare me?'

'Let me hold it first.'

'No. I found it.'

'Go on. Do it then.' Jabba puffed out his chest.

My finger traced the curve of the trigger. I'd never shot anything before.

'Chicken! Bwah bwah!' Jabba clucked. 'Girls don't shoot guns.'

I squeezed my eyes shut and pulled the trigger. The gun exploded in my hand. Bright lights whizzed in front of me. My ears rang. I thought I saw God.

'Faarrrk!'

The sky rumbled before we saw the police helicopter as it flew under grey clouds. I stuffed the gun in my backpack and started running through puddles and wet grass. Jabba ran after me, dragging his bike through the tall weeds of the creek embankment.

We took the side streets. Shortcuts through laneways and vacant blocks. There were cops everywhere. Sirens flashing blue on storefront windows. Hunting a gunman who'd shot up some cops the night before after they'd stopped and searched him. The cops didn't like that he had big guns and had gotten away. Anyone who had a Bulgarian-sounding name, which meant anyone with a Wog name, had their doors busted down. Houses and garages were searched while television journalists looked on with their video cameras pointed at the front doors.

By the time we got home, our white front gate was closed. We'd missed dinner. Dad would surely give us a hiding. We opened the gate, making sure the metal hinge didn't clang. Mum could hear a fart a kilometre away.

I opened my backpack.

'Could be the weapon he shot the cops with?' Jabba said, panting. Younger, he was always with the annoying questions.

'Prolly.'

'What do we do?'

I looked up and could just make out our Italian neighbour, Ralph, hiding behind his mum's hibiscus tree. This was in the days before Dad had erected a trellis along the boundary fence. We could see everything happening in their front garden and they could see what we were doing in ours. Ralph had no pants on. Just a Chips T-shirt so his doodle hung out in the wind. I couldn't help but stare. My cheeks were hot. It was the first willy I ever saw. He must've been cold, letting it hang like that on such a cold wintery day, as it was all shrivelled and gross. He was always sneaking around his front garden. Mum once caught him showing off his willy to our other neighbour, Mr Lim.

'It's not right,' Dad had said when he found out and gave Ralph's mother a talking to about it. But it didn't stop Ralph. He just did it more discreetly. Behind the camellia tree. Near the bins. Before Ralph's doodle-showing days, Dad called him "Papamosque" because his mouth was always open, catching flies like them Maltese flycatcher birds.

'Quick, we'll put it under the log.'

I crouched down, the hem of my dress dragging up the dirt. Beneath the log, the soil was alive with worms and those bugs that roll into a ball when you touch them. I scooped out the dirt, making a deep hole, placed the gun inside, and then Jabba put the log on top of it.

Ralph hung his face over the fence, watching. His mouth open.

'You better not tell.' Jabba flicked a stone at the fence. Ralph flinched.

I put my finger to my lips. 'Our secret, Ralph.'

He smiled.

***

We hid behind the sofa until Dad had calmed down and Mum said it was safe to come out. She microwaved our tea and ordered us to stay at the dinner table until every crumb was eaten off our plate. The steak was dry, the broccoli limp, so we knew we'd be sitting there for a while, chewing because Mum was watching us with her sharp blue eyes, a wooden spoon and chilli in hand the way her Burgher mum did when Mum was growing up in Sri Lanka.

Dad was still in his work shirt. His grease and sweat stunk up the room like a fish and chips shop. Silver armbands holding up his sleeves shimmered under the pale-yellow lights.

Eyewitness News blared from the TV's tinny speakers. The balding head of the gunman, which was shaped like a moon, flashed upon the screen. They were calling this on-the-run criminal the "Noble Park Gunman." Other channels called him "Mad Max," on account of his Anglo name, Max. His real name was Pavel Marinof, or something like that. But Australians couldn't pronounce it when he arrived in Australia so he changed his name to Max Clarke, a plain name that Australians could understand.

'This is Mad Max country,' Dad joked. He thought it was funny that Noble Park was on the news—our shitburb was rockstar famous.

'The cops might knock down our door,' I said, chewing the same piece of meat over and over. 'Or the Serbs up the street.'

'Could be hiding in our garage,' Jabba chimed in.

'Don't talk rubbish,' Mum shouted in her angry-thick Sri Lankan accent, and everyone went quiet.

School was called off because some teacher at a primary school found Mad Max's things in one of the portables. The cops reckoned someone was hiding him. I reckoned he was long gone by now. Dad was allowed to go to and from work but that was it. We were supposed to stay inside but Mum caught us sneaking out the next morning after breakfast. Jabba and I told her we were only going to play in the garage.

Every few minutes a helicopter flew over. The clouds were looking dirty—about to dump a tonne of rain. Jabba and I ducked into the garden, making sure Mum wasn't spying on us through the front window. She was always watching the neighbourhood, watching us or shouting at us to get off the street.

Jabba was ahead of me. Pulled up the log before I did with a grin so wide his cheeks could burst.

'Let's go looking for Mad Max.' He held up the gun. His small fingers could barely reach the trigger. He pointed it at our olive tree. At me.

'He'll shoot you,' I said. 'Shoot you like them cops.' I reached for the gun, but he smacked my hand away.

'Nah, he won't. We're Wogs like him.'

'Bullshit.'

Ralph stuck his doodle-looking head over the fence. He must've been waiting for us. 'What are you doing with that?' Ralph asked, his Papamosque mouth hanging open.

'I reckon we go look for him.' Jabba repeated and didn't wait for an answer. He took off, clanging the gate, which made Mum bang on the window at us in annoyance.

I threw my hands up in the air and ran after him. When I turned around, Ralph was running too. At least he had some pants on.

***

'Where we going?' Ralph dragged his feet behind us, wiping his nose. We stopped behind an old gumtree.

'Let's check out the school near the train station where they found his stuff. I betcha we catch him before the cops do,' Jabba said.

I protested but Jabba ignored me and cut across a vacant block. We followed. Ralph started to whinge about tall weeds and snakes. As we climbed the fence, my dress got caught on nails. I swore, 'Ḥaqq g̱ẖal-Madonna!' That's what Dad said when he was pissed off.

'Dad says girls shouldn't swear,' Jabba said.

'Up yours.' I flipped Jabba the bird.

We jumped into someone's backyard. A clothesline rotated with the wind, flapping sheets and undies.

'Maybe he's hiding in there?' I pointed to an outdoor dunny. 'No one would expect that.'

Ralph nodded but Jabba disagreed. 'Let's keep going.'

I reckoned Jabba was too gutless to look.

***

We didn't say anything until we reached Noble Park train station. Police cars were everywhere. We crossed the train tracks.

'Hey, you three. What are you doing here?' a cop called out from his car. There were a couple of Anglo boys, older than us, across the road from them, but they weren't getting called at.

'Nothing,' I squirmed.

'Come over here.' He wagged his finger at us like we'd done something wrong.

Jabba's and Ralph's eyes were lit with fear.

I decided to take charge. 'Run!'

We bolted. Hard. Those dirty clouds had finally unleashed. My dress was soaked through by the time we reached Ross Reserve. When Jabba slowed down, I jumped him for the gun and ran towards the creek. Ralph was way behind. When they finally caught up, I was sheltering under a river gum. We puffed our guts out once more as angry rain pelted us from all angles.

I looked down. There was a blanket. Someone was sleeping here. I caught a shadow.

'Oi!' The two boys from the tracks had followed us. 'Give us your money, Wogs.'

'We don't have any,' I barked.

'What you got in that bag?'

Jabba and Ralph moved closer to me. I recognised one of the boys. Adam. His dad was a cop. Adam used to bully me about the colour of my skin before he moved on to high school. He pulled out a knife.

'Give us the bag or we'll fuck your faces up.' Adam trod closer while his mate hung back. I reached into the plastic bag and pulled out the gun. Pointed it square at Adam's face. Adam laughed like it was some big joke. 'You're not going to shoot that thing?'

I cocked the gun like I did yesterday. 'Wanna make a bet?' My hands shook.

Adam had once chased me onto the road; I nearly got hit by a car. Another time, he pushed me off the monkey bars and I broke my arm. I thought of those things as I squeezed the gun.

Ralph jumped in front of me, laughing like a madman. 'She'll shoot ya!' He was Papamosque, a mouth-breather because his nose was all stuffed up. He unzipped his fly and pissed on Adam's Nikes. Adam threw a punch but Ralph ducked. I pulled the trigger.

The bullet missed Adam and hit the concrete drain. He turned red like he'd shat himself and took off with his mate. Adam looked back once as a helicopter flew low and whipped the branches and trees into a frenzy. 'Fucking Wogs! And you,' Adam shouted, pointing to the man behind us. 'You're dead when my dad finds out you're hiding 'ere.'

I caught the gunman's bald head as I dropped the gun. We ran.

Tadpole

Emma Bjorndahl

3rd Prize

The shiny brown skink stopped struggling. *Was it dead?* I leant forward on my elbows from my cool shaded nook under the prehistoric fern frond. I had been watching the skink struggle in the long blades of dry hot grass with its back legs wrapped tight in fine strands of web—reminding me of fairy floss.

I picked the lizard up to my eye level. I must look like a giant to the tiny skink nestled in the palm of my hand. The side of the lizard's neck was pulsing, but the rest of the reptile lay unmoving, delicately scaled toes glued together. I tried to unravel the web, plucking strands as gently as I could but becoming stickier as I worked. Sweat was beading around my hairline and I poked my tongue out.

The sun was white hot. I paused and looked over the lizard again; scales glistened and rippled in the light. The skink's neck stopped pulsing as I laid it on the ground among the sharp blades of grass where I had found it. The bound legs made me think the lizard had tried to shimmy into a tight skirt and got stuck. Sighing, I plucked a juicy-red hibiscus from above me, long stamen waving like antennae in the light breeze. I placed the flower over the body of the skink and sank to my knees—contemplating existence.

***

When it grew too hot, I stood up, escaping into the shade of a dilapidated garden shed. The shed housed my most precious possession: tadpoles. The shed's ancient plastic panelling and wooden beams were crumbling—all dry and splintered.

I stood on tiptoes at the sparse workbench, which was just a long beam of thick wood balanced against a wall. I peered into the murky water of a St Peter's-brand Neapolitan ice cream container. (Neapolitan ice cream was my favourite, except strawberry, which I always left for my younger brother.) I sniffed at the faint aroma of ice cream mixed with the smell of swamp water.

The tadpoles were all at different stages of development. Some were tiny, slimy black blobs with long, thick, clear tails. Others were fatter with stumpy tails and leg buds. As a general rule, my tadpoles turned into cane toads. I hoped this time it would be different. I had spent hours sifting through muddy water up to my waist, watching out for tiger snakes. At last, I had been rewarded with a nice fat clump of frogspawn. The clear bubbles were stuck together with promising black dots. Delighted, I had moved them to my ice cream container. Soon, I would fill the container with rocks, ready for the baby frogs to exit the water and take up residence in the garden.

***

I headed back to the house daydreaming of baby frogs. I paused in the open doorway. I could hear my parents' raised voices. Carefully, I leaned into the doorway and peered in. They were down the end of the hallway, shadow puppets dancing. I could hear them clearly now; they weren't just arguing, they were screaming at each other. I shivered; Mum would be sleeping downstairs in the spare room again. I didn't want to listen to it anymore.

I had one precious memory of us happy together. My brother and I were laughing and sliding down Dad's knees, Mum laughed with us. Eventually she stopped laughing, and sank into the bed, pulling the covers over her head. That was when the house was warm and bright.

Now it was dark and cold. After a fight with Dad, Mum would sit on the narrow day bed, her body pressed hard against the wall, as though she wanted to push through it. Legs pulled up under her chin, arms wrapped tight around her knees, shaggy brown curls hanging like stringy curtains over vacant eyes. If I felt brave, I would sit on the very end of the bed and watch her, or I would lie on the floor and quietly read. When she was in that state, she never spoke or looked at me. I thought of her like a beautiful, bright hibiscus flower that had fallen to the ground and become bruised and damaged.

***

What if I got out? What if I left? I could just pack a bag like I had seen them do a million times in old Disney cartoons. Donald Duck would wrap all his possessions in a large red and white spotted handkerchief and hang it from a stick, whistling as he left everything behind.

I rummaged through my wardrobe and found a small multicoloured backpack. It was full of stuffed toys. I tipped them out. *What else would I need?* There was a slender purple torch on my windowsill, which I used to study the ants that trooped through my window whenever it rained. *Still working.* I stuffed some clothes into the bag and made to leave—*My tadpoles!*

I dashed to the shed and carefully lifted the ice cream container off the rickety bench, trying not to spill water. The tadpoles were rocking in artificial waves, but they would be okay. I snuck down the side of the house and paused at our letterbox, looking up and down the well-vegetated street to make sure no one could see me. I turned left and hurried with my head down. Something whizzed past me. I heard a shout. I nearly dropped the tadpoles in surprise. Two scruffy local boys I hated were riding past. I poked my tongue out at their backs. *Ouch!* Bindis dug into my brown and callused feet. It had not occurred to me to wear shoes; no one ever did in small coastal towns. Eventually, I had to sit down on the side of the road to pluck the bindis out. I noticed the zip had burst on the bag from being too full. I carefully shoved the protruding clothes back in.

***

At last, I stood in front of enormous grey cement pipes. The pipes were stacked into a neat pyramid with one pipe placed at the very top like a Christmas tree star. The castle of pipes loomed above all the houses— conveniently stepped for climbing. Carefully, I placed the ice cream container on the top of the first pipe and then my bag. I stood on my tippy toes and hoisted myself up by my elbows, my skin scraping on the rough concrete.

Gentle sea air blew around as I laid my bursting backpack beside me. The tadpoles were safely nestled in my lap. Sitting in the top-most pipe, my legs swung out into nothingness. I felt I could breathe at last, even with my grazed elbows bleeding. I stared out over the rooftops all the way to the dark ocean horizon. The sky was turning dusky pink, soft cotton wool clouds drifted by, and I was free.

After a while, the ocean breeze became a blast, and the sky turned from soft pink to grey. I shivered, bare feet tucked under me. I rummaged through my bag; my jumper was gone! It must have fallen out along the way. Goosebumps were running up and down my arms and legs. I would have to go and look for the jumper, otherwise the wind and cold would chase me home. Nothing was going to stop me sleeping up here. I left my bag and tadpoles. 'I'll be back soon,' I promised.

I shimmied down the pipes, hurrying back along the path. I was nearly home before I saw the blue woollen jumper swinging from a low frangipani branch. The jumper must have caught as I walked past.

***

At the base of the pipes, I frowned as I noticed fresh bike tracks in the sand. I swung myself back up on my sore elbows, now cushioned by the soft woollen jumper. I pulled up into the top pipe and found to my horror an empty bag, clothes scattered, and the ice cream container gone.

Confused, I rummaged around the piles of clothes. In relief, I finally felt the firm handle of my torch; it was getting dark. I clicked the torch on and spread the beam around the pipe. There were two sets of damp footprints; someone had been here recently. My stomach tightened.

Puddles glistened in the beam of light and the ice cream container lay on its side a little further down. Those ratbag boys on the bikes had seen me climb up here! They must have kicked the ice cream container around the pipe and stepped on the tadpoles making them pop, the insides spewing out.

I knelt down among the crushed and broken bodies, tears mingled with my snot; they were all dead. Slowly, I moved the beam around, but there was no hope. I stuffed my clothes back into the bag, sobbing and wiping my nose with the clean sleeve of my jumper. It seemed pointless, but I picked up the ice cream container and gazed inside. A pool of water was caught in one corner of the container. I shone my torch and squinted my eyes. A tiny wriggling black body emerged for a moment in the light. I gasped in relief. One. One had survived. I carefully made my way back down the pipes and bolted home.

***

'It will probably be another cane toad,' Mum said with suspicion as we surveyed the last surviving tadpole. It was thriving; the tail had shrunk down to a stump. *Not this time,* I was confident. *This will be the one.* I knew I would finally get a frog. *Soon,* I gloated. It felt good that Mum was finally taking an interest. She had listened to me sobbing out my story and had been indignant on my behalf.

'Come quick,' Mum said, her eyes bright. I ran outside with her. In dismay, I saw that the ice cream container was sitting exposed on the garden table near the shed. 'Oh, it's gone.'

There was nothing but a little wet patch on top of the rock. Mum looked at me, eyes wide. 'It was a green tree frog!'

I heard a noise and saw a heavy black crow clinging to a branch above us. My heart sank. I knew the frog was gone. I had to quell the urge to yell at Mum. To ask why she had moved the ice cream container from the safety of the shed and brought it out in the open. 'It was here!' She lifted up the container to look underneath it.

I hid my sorrow. 'Don't worry, Mum. It probably just hopped away.'

'Do you think so?' she asked, putting her arm around my shoulders. It felt nice.

'Yeah,' I said, leaning into her.

First Impressions

Jessie Lambert

Highly Commended

'Fuck!' I shout, snatching my hand back from the steel pan handle. I race to the sink, banging on the cold-water tap. Inspecting the damage, I find my middle and pointer fingers branded red. *Great, that's my two good fingers! Just what I need for a hot date.*

I would have grabbed the oven mitts, but they could be anywhere. I probably left them on the couch or in the fridge. *Who knows!* I haven't even started cooking the special spaghetti yet and I am already injured. *Typical.*

I glance down at my watch. Hot Date Rachel will be here in an hour. My first date since Alex. Bile rises from my stomach. *Why the heck did I suggest a first date at my house?* It has "I'm a Hot Mess" littered all over.

See, Hot Date Rachel is my soul mate. I know this because my psychic told me just this week and, so far, she has been eerily right about everything. Last year, she foretold the day of my grandmother's death, down to what she was wearing (her flamboyant Nanna nightie) and her last words said to me (which were basically stop being so gay and produce more children instead—said with love). My psychic also foretold that my heart would break on my birthday this year (and it did, surprise!). So when my psychic speaks, I listen.

'But!,' I remember the psychic saying, waving her pointed finger toward my eye, making me jump out of my cushion, 'You will have only *one* chance to impress her. If you fail to impress, the cards say you either risk being alone for a long time or you will find yourself only in relationships that refuse to see your quirks as the gift they are ... which is pretty much the same thing.'

I have one chance. I cannot, by any means, let on how much I fail at being a fully grown adult. No mess. No forgetfulness. No reveal of my real self. *Where do I even begin?* I automatically reach for my phone to message Alex. She would know what to do. But no, this is for a *date*. And anyway, we aren't talking. Going on four weeks now. Four long weeks I've had to figure out life on my own. I wanted independence and now I have it. *Yay for me?*

I let out a groan as I slide down the pantry door until I'm sitting on the cold floor. *Why didn't I cook this meal sooner? Must I leave everything to the very last minute? How can I tidy this all up in time?* I hear a cackling and the smell of burning oil. *Wait, I was in the middle of cooking already!* I run to the pan—it spits hot oil onto my chest. *Ouch! Why did I say I would make my special spaghetti? Where was that recipe again?*

I reach for my phone to message Alex. We made it together so many times and she always reminded me of what goes in when. Even though it was *my* family recipe. Well, she was Italian after all, with that velvety olive skin, striking green eyes, and hair dark in tight short curls. How can her skin be so soft, melting like butter in my hands that made her shiver every time I slid them up the nape of her neck. And those soccer legs: strong and thick. Easy to grab onto when I needed to … direct. Alex, who was the calm to my confusion, would often joke: 'How would you do anything without me, babe?' To which my reply would always be: 'I would not survive this cruel and practical world.' I chop the onion, my eyes wet before I even begin to slice.

Okay, deep breaths. One chop at a time. That's what Alex would say. Next up is the celery. Celery … Oh shit, celiac! Rachel is celiac! I glance up from the cutting board, eyes wide, accidentally slicing too forcefully and narrowly missing my finger. I look at my watch. Thirty minutes to go. I need gluten-free pasta. *What a disaster. I am a disaster. This night needs to be perfect. Good impression. One chance.*

I grab my keys and run to the car. *Supermarket here I come!* Beep, beep, beep. The engine light shines its smug orange light at me. *Oh, that's right! I need oil because of that oil leak I've been meaning to get fixed.* I don't drive far because my car always overheats. It's summer, so driving with the heater on high is unbearable. *If only I called the mechanic and had him check the leak! How embarrassing! I don't have time to buy oil. What oil would I buy anyway?* Alex would know. Alex would have called the mechanic for me already. Alex would have reminded me. I head back to the kitchen.

Alex was celiac too. *Is that my type? Ha!* I could ask her. I know she has pasta by the boxful, being Italian and all. She said to ask if I ever needed anything. She knew I needed help to human. *One* chance. *I'm going to message her. It's for a very practical emergency!* Surely, my ex doesn't want me to be alone forever.

I reach into my pocket for my phone. Empty. I freeze, wide-eyed. *Could be anywhere!* I look up and presented in front of me is the week's worth of dishes still piled up on the sink … no phone.

While searching for my phone, I go over what I would write to Alex: *Hey! Any chance I could borrow some gluten-free pasta like right now? It's a pasta emergency.* My hands are sweaty, heart now beating out of my chest. *I still need to cook! Dining room?* I lift the pile of papers on the dining table, which accidentally tip over the washing basket on the edge of the table, toppling all over the floor. I could write: *'Hey! I've been meaning to message you … how have you been? How is your new girlfriend? I have been doing so great. Better than ever! Could I borrow some GF pasta?'* No, no I can't message Alex. We aren't talking for a reason.

Next, I scan the lounge area and notice that piles of old National Geographic magazines, cuttings, and off-cuts from my unfinished art project idea last week are littered on the coffee table. *Yet another unfinished project. Why do I even bother?* Alex would usually come and help me with getting organised. *Ah, there it is!* On the couch. Right next to the oven mitts.

On my phone I open Messenger and type: 'Hey you … Can I please borrow some gluten-free spaghetti of yours? I'll give you a penne for your efforts! :)' Unease invades my stomach. I hit send.

I finish the special spaghetti from what I remember: mince, tomatoes, olives, red wine. I swig from the bottle. Warm and soothing as it slides down. Easing my nerves. *A splash for me. A splash for you. Oops!*

I stir the red saucy pot. *Who serves pasta without pasta?* I scoop some up; it's runnier than usual. *And now it's pasta soup! What will Hot Date Rachel think of me? She will probably be polite, say, 'Oh, thank you for my weird pasta!' and leave as soon as possible.*

I check my phone. The message is still unread. *What do I do? I guess we can order pizza. I did say I was making her my specialty dinner though … which is why we aren't out at a restaurant. Amazing, what a great first impression this is! I know, I'll message her and say I am coming down with a cold and need to raincheck, which isn't far from the truth.* Between failing at dinner and texting my ex, my stomach feels like a circus. I look at my watch: 6 pm. Too late for the raincheck option.

Knock, knock, knock. *Great and Hot Date Rachel punctual, ugh!*

'Hi!' Rachel exclaims, out of breath. Her face lights up with excitement. She is stunning: wavy, wild brown hair and a short choppy fringe, golden hazel eyes, and deep red lips ... that continues across her cheek? *Interesting.*

I follow the red line and see sweet pink duck earrings (probably handmade) and a bold red waratah flower tattoo stretching across her right shoulder. The tattoo flows into a mismatched sleeve of tattoos including skulls, music notes, quotes, more ducks, a snake wrapping around her forearm, and on three fingers are the capital letters Y-E-S. And of course, very, very short nails. Like, extremely short. *Oh, that's right, guitarist nails. I am on a date with an actual musician who is smoking hot! Shame I've already fucked it up. I'm a sweaty mess without a tattoo in sight!*

'I'm sorry I'm late. I was so excited texting you this week that I thought we said six o'clock, not five o'clock. I only realised half an hour ago and then I couldn't remember if I told you I was celiac, so I stopped to buy some gluten-free bread on the way. I had no idea what the 'special' dinner was, so I thought: "Bread goes with everything!" but then I left my phone at home so I couldn't text you to say I was late and then I saw I didn't have petrol so I had to go find a petrol station and because I was so worried about being late I missed my turnoff. But I'm here!' Rachel says, smiling and holding up a bag of bread.

I notice she is wearing all black: platform Doc Martin boots, flowy pants, and a dangerously low-cut collared sleeveless shirt ... with a white strip of toothpaste running down the front? *Ha, relatable.* And Hot Date Rachel's arms are surprisingly muscular. *That arm could seriously push me up against this wall. Must be all that strumming.* I bite my lip at the thought.

'You aren't late, we said 6 pm, perfect timing.' I sigh with a smile. 'You are perfect.' I stand there mesmerised. 'Come in. I'm sorry, I forgot you are celiac and I didn't buy gluten-free pasta. How does spaghetti sauce on toast sound?'

'Yes! Spaghetti soup!' Rachel exclaims. Rachel steps inside, spots herself in the mirror, and gasps. 'Oh my gosh, I am so embarrassed! I put lipstick on when I stopped at the lights and I totally forgot to check it.

I wanted to appear cool and put together for you. Instead, I look like a clown. Not the best first impression!' Rachel says, then turns to the mirror, licks her fingers, and scrunches up her face to sand back the wandering lipstick.

Rachel turns, searching my eyes as if to gauge what I'm thinking. I'm staring at her through the mirror, head tilted and eyes glazed over. 'The most gorgeous clown I've ever seen,' I say, head swaying side to side. Wait, did I just say she looks like a gorgeous clown? What is wrong with me? We both laugh in nervous concert.

Rachel moves her eyes around, looking at the laundry on the chair and spilling onto the floor. I see her looking past me at the fallen sprawling magazines and cuttings over the floor. Oh no, I forgot to clean up the house! I hold my breath. I'm sure she wants to run.

'Oh, thank god you aren't super tidy. I don't think we would get along otherwise. That's one of my red flags actually, being too neat. A house is for living in!'

I let out the longest sigh. 'Excuse me one second, I need to do something real quick.'

Dash to my phone. Message is still unseen. *Phew.* Delete.

Lowanna's Fever

Adam Brannigan

Highly Commended

The four of us were camping at Massacre Bay over the long weekend. Just the boys. Drinking, fishing, and surfing. Second night in and we were well into our third or fourth round of Waru's homebrew. We'd been telling stories, looking into the fire, and then Djalu said, 'Yeah, I got one.'

Course he did. He was the kind of bloke who always had a story and always went one better. Half of what he said, half of the time, were outright lies. So, when Uncle Crow finished his story about a shapeshifting hitchhiker, we knew Djalu was gonna chime in next. He'd been champing at the bit.

'Me great-grandma told us this one when we was kids.' Djalu's voice was a deep rumble. As if a mountain were speaking. As if stones were grinding on stones. He was tall, heavy-set, rooted to the earth. All his family were like that; they were built big and strong, with thunder in their voices. His father and grandfather were famous veterans of the '67 eradication. Before that they used to track and hunt the Gubba that escaped from the mission. No one ever got away from them. You didn't mess with Djalu or his family. So, even though he always stretched the truth, we showed him respect.

We drank and kept our tongues, while Djalu let the silence gather in the spaces between us. We could hear the surf and the sovereign stone curlews calling out weer-lo, weer-lo in the dunes. The moon lit up the paperbarks before the clouds closed in and made everything outside of our camp dark again. One of the hardwood offcuts in the fire drum hissed and spat savage sparks at us. 'She reckoned every word of it was true as.'

Course she did. Whenever we went camping and had a few, we'd tell stories about the strange things we saw on the road or in the bush, out at sea—things we could never explain. Usually, after we'd set up camp, and had a feed, we'd light the fire drum, start on the piss, yarn about life. Then, we'd talk about *those* moments—about the hungry Ngayurnangalk and Malpu, or the long-ago dead and their hauntings. We thought we'd heard all of Djalu's stories, but he'd never mentioned his great-grandmother before.

'My great-grandmother's name was Lowanna. When she was a kid, her family lived on a ceded property near Gundy. They'd claimed it during the Frontier Wars and kept growing the wheat planted by the Gubba. I think they maybe had a decent number of cattle as well. But when Lowanna was young, they hadn't started to round the Invaders up and put them on the missions yet. Treaty was still in place. They kept a few on as farmhands and servants and she reckoned it was mostly peaceful in them days. It was the next generation that caused all the trouble, she reckoned. Too high and mighty.'

We all knew our history. We all know how it ended for the Whitefellas. Djalu was just stretching out his moment. Too much of a showman that one.

'When she's about sixteen or so it starts. She senses someone's in the room with her. She smells burning hair. She tells her parents. They don't believe her. She sleeps in their bed, or with her sisters, but it don't matter. Whatever the *thing* is, *it* follows her. Nobody else notices the burning smell and they don't wake up in a lather like she does. It doesn't happen every night, but it happens a lot. Too often, she reckoned.' Djalu let the silence breathe. The wind shifted and blew the smoke from the fire amongst us.

***

June 23rd, 1913. It happened again last night. I was in my own bed and woke with a start, soaked with fear. I knew immediately that it was in the room. I could hear it moving around, and in the air hung the same strong smell that had been present on other occasions. It was exactly as burnt hair, entirely unmistakable. Whatever it was stopped moving, and I knew at once that it was standing next to my bed, but as I was safely under the covers, I daren't look. I suppose I must have fallen asleep at some point.

***

'This goes on for a few weeks. She reckons she started getting sick of near suffocating every time it turns up, so she decides to look one night.'

***

July 9th, 1913. If it visits tonight, then I will face it.

***

We sat deeper into our camp chairs. Looked into the fire. Looked into the shadows. Looked into the night sky—hoping not to see anything strange. Djalu's words had put the wind up us. Then Waru, who always listened closely but never told his own stories, broke the spell and asked too loudly, 'Eh, Djalu, whichway?'

'Yeah, okay. So, she looks out into her room.' He paused, again.

'Yeah, and?' Waru again, getting annoyed onetime.

Uncle Crow was hidden in the depths of his camp chair. His scrawny legs and bare feet the only thing of him that was visible. Also annoyed, Uncle Crow asked, 'C'mon Djalu, stop muckin' about. What'd she see?'

***

But I have asked the ancestors to protect me.

***

'A man. An old Whitefella soldier in full battle kit from Invasion times. But messed up.'

I asked how without thinking and regretted it straight-up—not really wanting to know what Djalu meant by messed up.

'He was burnt bad. That was the smell she'd been smelling. Half his face was gone, melted away, dripping. And not only that, he had smoke coming off of him, like he was still burning. His mouth open like he was screaming.' Bloody hell. We took that in. Waru muttered something to himself and Djalu half-smiled. He had us; hook, line and sinker. 'Yeah, it's pretty grim.'

Djalu bloody Djalu. Always going one better than the rest of us. We stayed put. No one got up to piss. No one got up to add more wood to the fire. No one got up to get more beer.

Djalu continued, 'It's too much for Lowanna and she screams and wakes up the whole house. She's in a real state and they can't calm her down. She wants them all to leave the house, the farm, everything, give it back to the Gubba, go back into the scrub, back to the old ways, believing the place is cursed. They have to hold her down and tie her to the bed and she fights like the devil. Her mother, my great-great grandmother, is bawling her eyes out. Lowanna's sisters are screaming the house down. But she's trussed up. Sometime during the night she develops a fever. She's close to death. One of the Gubba farmhands goes and gets the lore man and the doctor.'

'Did she die?' I asked, expecting Djalu to pause. But he's on a roll and answers straight-up.

'Nah, brother. It takes her a few weeks, but Lowanna, yeah, she pulls through. But she's not really the same after that. Talking all funny and staring at nothing for hours on end. Real womba. Her dad decides that it's time to ship her off, out of the way. Get her healed or get her gone. So, he and a couple of the strongest farmhands took her as far as the railhead at Wallangarra and then a family friend took her from there to Toowoomba and then down the range to Ipswich and into Old Gallup.'

***

August 5th, 1913. My family are heartless monsters. Should I run away?

***

'She reckoned she was this close to running away, but knew she wouldn't get far, even on horseback. She's still weak and her lungs kinda shot and she's pretty sure no one in the district will shelter her. On her last night at home, she cries herself to sleep. But that night, he comes back.'

Waru asked, 'What, the dead Whitefella?'

Djalu shifted forward in his camp-chair and scratched his leg. 'Yep. This time she wakes up and sees him by her bed. She's not scared, but. She used to say to us kids it's because she was close to dying and the fever took her fear away. The ghost walks out of her bedroom. He's leading her somewhere, for sure. She gets out of bed and follows him through the house, lighting a lamp on the way. They go through the yard to one of the sheds, or barns, or whatever. When she goes inside, the ghost is standing near a stack of crates and stuff, so she begins to open them crates one by one.' Djalu paused. The final moments of the burning hardwood, the night's hush, a gemmed sky invited a few moments of silence.

After a while, Uncle Crow said, 'What'd she find, Djalu?'

'Well, Uncle, after a bit, she opens a wooden box and takes out what's in it. She sees smooth curves … jagged edges … holes. Great-grandma Lowanna said she felt sick touching it. She put it right back.'

We knew what she'd found. Djalu didn't have to tell us.

'But she still picks up the lamp and the wooden box and follows the old Whitefella soldier to one of the trees near the house. He gets on his knees, lays his battle kit aside and begins clawing at the ground.'

I asked, 'Did they bury it, Djalu?'

***

August 3rd, 1933. That night, those many years ago, are still somewhat hazy as if covered in smoke. The vestiges of the fever? Was I truly awake? What of it is imagination? What parts real? Only I can tell the whole of it. While near the oak, I heard my name being shouted and can recall Father running toward me, revolver in hand. Behind him the others of my family summoned from sleep. Everything moved slowly as if we were all somehow suspended in water. Father, with his great strength, gathered me up while firing into the now-empty night. His momentum knocked everything from me. The box fell from my hands, opening on the way to the ground. The brittle bone broke upon it and released a thousand small curses into the dense atmosphere. The lamp, cast-free, set the whole night on fire.

It Begins

Grace Buckley

Local Award

Two snakes are intertwined at the base of a riverbed and are sliced in half with the strike of a shovel. The snakes wriggle and writhe until they come to a stop, only to be nudged into the water to drift down the stream. It's October; *it's beginning.*

***

Andrea can feel it in the morning, the sudden change in season. She can smell it in the stench of her grandmother's peonies wafting through the open bedroom window, mixing with something burnt. The approaching summer heat meant thick smoke and ash descended the mountains and into the valley at a regular occurrence. Multiple times a week, the town of Yallambee's backdrop lit up in hues of glowing orange come nightfall—a series of backburning to ensure the town's rural landscape is kept safe from dry months and long sunny days.

Andrea kicks the top sheet off the end of her bed and drags herself to the kitchen. Nan has left a smiley face and an affirmation scrawled on the chalkboard fridge. Her grandfather's empty coffee mug sits at the edge of the sink, abandoned at the first sight of dawn in order to move his herd of cattle to drink from the river.

Andrea twists the cold tap on and the water runs warm out of the faucet. It leaves her hot and her face flushed red as she washes the night away. The day ahead is looking meek. Evidently, she wants to be eleven again, swaddled in a soaking towel with her little brother pressed beside her. Their hair wet from chlorine as they'd wait at the only takeaway store in Yallambee. Twenty dollars clasped in Andrea's fist, the siblings would squabble about potato scallops and Chicko rolls.

Instead, Andrea swelters as she walks from the employee carpark beside the old timber mill and up to the back dock of Thompson's Grocer. The distance is short but the long black pants of her uniform stick to her skin with sweat. It's 9 am and she's already sick with it.

'Andy! Nice of you to show up.' The Deli Supervisor greets Andrea with a Cheshire smile and twinkle in their eye.

'I could leave?' Andrea jokes, pretending to turn toward the door she had just slipped through. They laugh and exchange pleasantries before Andrea trudges up the stairs toward the staffroom in search of air-conditioning and the half-empty Redbull she left in the fridge.

***

By lunch, Andrea's hands are red. Her skin is dry and cracked. Her palms itch but she restrains herself by clawing her nails into her thighs through the fabric of her pants.

The town is miserable, smoked out and spread thin. Most spend the day strewn out in front of their air-con with their windows tightly shut. While the less fortunate chase the breeze of a fan or brave the smoky landscape to cool themselves in rivers the colour of iced tea.

It's grown hotter with each hour that has passed. Andrea can see the wear it has had on her neighbours as they slump through the grocery store doors. Word has got around that three major fires have gotten out of control. The state firefighters, their volunteers and the rural brigades containing farmers, tradesmen, and the usual retirees—all come through at different intervals. Dirt cakes each of their faces and charcoal stains their clothes. Bedraggled, dehydrated, and tired from fighting blazes that burn long and strong.

***

Thompson's Grocer boxes up snacks, bottled water, and Gatorade to send out to the troops. Cool cans of Coke and lemonade are tipped into icy eskies and sent with them when they pitstop for petrol or load up on water storage. Andrea offers the firefighters a smile as she buys her own Powerade and slinks out the back.

'They've called in all the fire trucks from other LGAs and there's three helicopters at the showground,' the Store Manager says, pressing a cold water bottle to her forehead. A group of Andrea's co-workers sit on empty milk crates in the cool room, scrolling community Facebook pages for updates while methodically rehydrating.

'All the rural brigades are up in Port Pot, fighting the blaze on that hill behind the hospital.'

'Shit, that's risky,' the Butcher sighs beside Andrea. 'Put all their eggs in one basket with that one.'

Andrea nods in agreeance, leans against the refrigerated wall, closes her eyes and stretches her legs. One of Andrea's fellow cashiers nudges her knee with their own and places an ice block in her lap. Andrea feels the sting of its frozen form through her clothes and desperately wishes she could lie down on the icy floor of their walk-in freezer forevermore.

**

There are words that sit fat on Andrea's tongue and weigh heavily. Yet, she cannot swallow the words down without gagging for air. She wants to ask the people she knows and who know her, her colleagues printed on roster sheets and with printed name badges. The colleagues who smile when they see her. Andrea wants their advice. A matchbox is in her hand but she's unwilling to strike the match.

Because as the season is changing, so too is Andrea. Come summer, when the transition has settled, Andrea may no longer wake to peonies outside her windows. Instead, there would be just concrete at her doorstep. Andrea is nervous. She does not wish to leave, but the pressure is becoming too much, and her grandmother is insisting.

'I think it's time, my love,' Nan had said, sitting beside Andrea on her bed. Nan squeezed Andrea's knee in comfort. Andrea did not ask for her grandfather's opinion; he already told Andrea that he hadn't expected to suffer through another drought in his lifetime. Andrea knew how he felt about survival as a necessity and what it means to stay.

The offer to leave town had come from her brother, who had fled two years beforehand. This was back when the sky was grey and the grass was green.

**

Andrea thinks about her brother as she works. She flits from one side of the store to the other, completing tasks and chatting as she goes.

Andrea's brother had no opposition to leaving as he was too excited. Andrea almost didn't cry when he disappeared down the driveway. She'd almost forgotten that she was losing something, having been caught up in his infectious energy.

Andrea didn't feel that way when he'd texted her three weeks ago about a new apartment and an empty room. She felt as sweaty as she did now, hauling trolleys through the carpark, waving to passers-by as she went. She wonders if it's time to let go.

Clocking out, Andrea drags herself to the staffroom balcony that overlooks the town and watches the mountains burn. She stands beside her friends, witnessing the fire consume everything it touches and choking the valley in thick smoke ruin.

Unable to stand the sight of her hometown aflame, Andrea slinks away. She wishes her co-workers a goodbye and takes off into the afternoon sun, vacating through the same door she trudged through nine hours earlier.

The heat in her small four-door is stifling when she unlocks it and slides into the driver's seat. Andrea lets her mind drift while her body drives, autopilot steering her in the direction of fast-flowing rapids that are hidden behind thick tree coverage on the border of town.

Andrea's tyres tread through dead grass and flatten the browning ground as she rolls through to the river. It's secluded and the only sound Andrea hears when she climbs through the bushland is the rush of water and the call of the birds high in the trees. Only a few locals knew of its existence and Andrea had learnt all of Yallambee's secrets long, long ago.

Slipping off her pants and unbuttoning her blouse, Andrea leaves them folded on shore. The body of a brown snake laps at the edge of the water; Andrea only spares it a glance. It's cool when she sinks in. Her earlobes graze the surface. The cold has her by the throat, second to the smoky haze of the afternoon.

Andrea wades for a while as she lets herself float and think—drowning out the sounds of the outside with submersion and diversion. She counts birds in the sky and watches as daylight starts to dim, ignoring the ash in the air. Her skin prunes and the chill creeps further into her bones, making her lips quiver. Hours have passed and her bra is waterlogged (ruined for the next working day) yet she remains afloat. If Andrea stayed here forever, then she would never have to choose. Nothing could touch her.

The burnt orange sunset peaks through the pillars of smoke; it cannot rival the red of the hills. Andrea watches it from the rocky bank of the river swaddled in an old towel. Her hair hangs wet and stringy. She is alone. She does not want to leave. Time is a shovel and it is splitting her in half. These hills are her home so she eventually must burn the land to the ground in order to prepare for a future.

The Calling

Kate O'Connor

Local Award

Daz sprawled across the wrinkled leather sofa. His knobbly heels dangled loosely off the end, soles of his feet grey with grit. *Grubby old bastard.* Daz's mesh basketball shorts had big baggy leg holes, which allowed his sunburnt thighs to splay comfortably as the fan clacked above his head. Clack, clack, clack.

Daz made no attempt to move over for me, despite the fact I was taxiing an icy cold can of Solo from the fridge to the couch for him. 'Just put it on the ground Ronny-roo,' he said, not taking his eyes off the television. Daz only ever called me "Ronny-roo" when I was doing him a favour. I put the can down next to a discarded Slurpee cup where a red plastic spoon-straw lay to the right and a trickle of Kermit-green coloured syrup interconnected the two across the carpet. I trailed my eyes up to the television. A girl about my age with hair blonder than fuzz on a peach effortlessly surfed a breaking wave in a neon-pink G-string bikini. The camera cut to all-male commentators that looked like a pack of alley cats ogling a fishbowl. I looked down at Daz. He held a similar googly-eyed gaze at the television screen.

'You're really into surfing now, ay?' I asked.

'Yeah, surfing is rad.'

'Even for girls?'

'Ken oath! Female surfers are hot as.'

'Yeah,' I said. 'I think I'm meant to be a surfer.'

Like a trek to the servo after a night on the tins, finding my path in life was a punishing journey. Back in high school, Mrs Clagg, the careers counsellor who was also the geography teacher, gave it a shot. In the end, Mrs Clagg conceded that nothing was really jumping out at her since I didn't have any notable hobbies or skills—unless she counted the fact I could eat a Golden Gaytime without spilling a single biscuit crumb. Mum said if I got my lips done, I could marry a rich bloke, because that's what she wishes she'd done. Instead, Mum ended up with a plumber who was never at home to fix his own leaks because he was always out trying to stick his pipe elsewhere—according to her.

I didn't know any rich blokes, but Daz reckoned he'd be rich one day with the amount of Keno he played. Until then, he was meant to be doing his electrician apprenticeship, but most days he just watched sport on the telly. I didn't mind watching a bit with him now and then. Good bonding time. Plus, it set my path! When I saw that surfer gliding along my television, something hit me. I could do that. I didn't have a fancy G-string bikini, but it doesn't cost anything to yank your cozzie up between your bum cheeks.

My younger brother, Troy, was an ace surfer. His surfboard was signed by Kelly Slater and everything. He reckoned that bit of scribble added hundreds to the resale value. Not that he would ever sell it. The board was his pride and joy. So, it was especially generous of him to lend it to me to practice on. Well, he wasn't home when I called, but I was only going to borrow it for a couple of hours. Mum said I'd better put it back before he got home from the pub or all hell would break loose.

'Yeah, yeah. Goes without saying,' I said.

I carried Troy's board the whole way down to the beach from Mum's place with the sun hammering away at my back. By the time my feet squeaked onto the soft sand, sweat had cast an almighty shadow on my swimmers. I put the board down on the sand and lay on top of it, one ear pressed to the smooth fibreglass while I caught my breath. I could smell the salt mist as it flew into the air with every tossed wave, dusting over my clammy skin like chicken salt on a hot chip. Facing the ocean, I rested my chin on the front of the board, feeling the grains of sand moving underneath me. I paddled with my hands as I started fanning sand downward. I pushed up to my knees and then to my feet with arms outstretched. I was ready.

I picked up Troy's board, slung it under my arm and jogged to the shoreline. As I cushioned my heels in the wet sand, the pale green waves frothed and frilled at my feet encouragingly. I untangled the leg rope and heaved the board in the water. Before I could attach the untangled leg rope to my ankle, an errant wave—a thieving bully of a bastard—muscled in.

43

Without warning, the wave gobbled up Troy's board and spat it out past my reach. Oh boy, did I panic. I started swimming toward the board as fast as I could, but I was pummelled by four big waves in a row. I tossed and turned and when I finally surfaced, the neat barrelling waves were replaced by washing machine white froth. No board in sight.

***

The sun had disappeared over the hill by the time I emerged from the water. I cupped my fists over my eyes like hand binoculars, but I still couldn't see the surfboard anywhere. I clambered to the top of the sand dunes then kept going until I reached the headland, where a cliff jutted out forty-five degrees like a piece of broken ceramic. "The Widow Maker" the locals called it because of an unfortunate buck's party incident back in the nineties. At the peak is a car park with a couple of splintery and old wooden benches sandwiched by scrubland. The only cars that ever went up there were filled with bong-smoking and horny teenagers like my brother. I knew that because "TROY MILES WOZ HERE" was scratched into one of the benches.

'Troy is going to farken' kill me,' I muttered. Again, I looked out at the darkened waves and dimming sky.

I guess I was a bit hidden by the scrubland because an approaching van definitely didn't see me. The van was a shiny black Mercedes transporter emblazoned in a swanky gold logo with interlinked Cs on the side panels. Carpet Castle.

A chunky man in his late forties with wavy hair as dark as a Bundy and Coke and a gold earring in each ear got out of the driver-side door. I recognised him from the telly. The Carpet Castle advertisement played on repeat during every footy game: 'For the best carpet in town, all hail the Carpet King!' In the ad, Carpet King wore a plastic gold crown and pointed a sceptre at the slashed prices on the screen. In person, he was puffed and shiny—as embalmed as the roast chicken Mum forgot to take out of the oven last Christmas.

Carpet King tilted his head from left to right, his eyes darting as he scuttled around to the back of his van and opened both doors. Leaning into the van, Carpet King let out a hurling dry retch. I'm a sympathetic vomiter, so the sound nearly got me going too. With a loud grunt, Carpet

King pulled a rug toward him until it landed on the ground. It was one of those fancy Persian rugs all tightly rolled up and bound in sections with duct tape. It must've been heavy because it looked as thick as Troy's pet python after it accidentally ingested his footy boot back in high school. At each end of the rug, I could see a bit of a black and swishy rubbish bag. It took Carpet King a few minutes of pushing, tugging and rolling before he got the roll to the precipice and then: Boom. Gone.

Carpet King wiped his brow and flicked sweat onto the grass. As he turned around, he made eye contact with me. 'Oh fuck,' he said. He looked down at the grass and grimaced. There was a long flat patch where he had dragged the rug to the edge. He stamped his foot around to fluff the grass back up. 'Listen carefully,' he growled. 'I was just getting rid of an old rug, alright?'

When I got home, I told Daz the whole story. 'Shit Ronda,' he said. 'That surfboard is going to cost you a bomb to replace. It was signed by Kelly Slater and everything.'

It got me thinking. There must be some decent money in the rug industry if the Carpet King didn't even think twice about chucking that fancy rug off the headland. Maybe the whole thing was actually a sign that I should get into the rug industry.

***

The next day, Daz gave me a lift down to Carpet Castle. The place smelled exactly like the pine tree car freshener I hung off the rear-view mirror of my Barina. Royal Pine-O scent. Carpet King was sitting in the back corner at a grey plastic desk with two computer screens.

'Hello, your highness,' I said.

He sized me up with his eyes. 'Yes?'

'Do you have any jobs going?'

'Do you have sales experience?' he asked.

'No,' I said.

'Got a boyfriend?'

'Yes.'

'Then no,' he replied and turned away from me.

'Why did you roll that rug off the Widow Maker?' I asked. 'Is it because you're rich?'

Carpet King spun his chair back around. His eyebrows shot up and down in rapid succession, moulding his eyes into meaty slits. 'Are you blackmailing me?' he hissed.

I looked down at the desk between us which lay peppered with royal spittle. 'No,' I said.

'Get out!' he bellowed. 'I am the North Coast's king of carpets. I don't have time for these antics!'

When I got back to the car, Daz was watching the motocross on my phone.

'Troy called looking for you,' he said, not looking up.

I froze. 'Shit. You didn't tell him I lost his board, did you?'

'Didn't need to. He's in the clink. Apparently a rug with a dead body inside surfed it into Long Mile Beach this morning.'

'You're bloody joking!'

He shook his head. 'Nope.'

'Cripes,' I said. 'You'd better drop me to the cop shop then.'

'Well, I can't wait around Ronda,' Daz said. 'I have to be at the pub at six. If I miss the start of a round, I'll have to buy me own beers all night.'

***

By the time I arrived, Troy was sweating bullets. I was glad the coppers were there while I was explaining the whole thing, otherwise I reckon Troy would've throttled me dead on the spot. When I finished, the cops looked at each other and smiled. 'Holy shit,' one said to the other. 'That Carpet King wanker is finally done for.'

About a week later, the cops came and knocked at my door. Gave Daz a real big fright, which set him off stuttering about how the ciggies accidentally fell into his pocket at Spiro Theodopolis's dad's IGA. Then the cops told Daz they were looking for me. He laughed really loudly and said he was just mucking around and he definitely didn't steal any Winnie Dark Blues from Spiro's dad last week. Such a joker, old Daz.

The cops came into the lounge room. 'You're going to want to be sitting down Ronda,' one of them said.

Once I sat down, they gave me the good news. The dead bloke in the carpet was a rival shop owner who had been missing for a few weeks. In an effort to find him, his family had put up a fifty-thousand dollar reward for information leading to an arrest. I couldn't believe it.

'Well, shit,' I said. 'I'll have to keep that quiet or Troy will come looking for a new surfboard.'

The detective said, 'That was good work, Ronda. You ever think about becoming a cop?'

Mojo

Ingrid Woodrow

Local Award

No one batted an eyelid when, at the tender age of thirty-seven, I announced my retirement.

'Retiring from what? It's not like you do anything anyway,' my sister said, puffing smoke rings and swigging Bundy and Coke. She wasn't wrong. But I'd lost my mojo. It was hard work just getting out of bed each morning. 'At least Newcastle has actual beaches. You can work on getting a *real* tan,' she continued, grimacing as she drained her can of pre-mix and looked disapprovingly at my forearms which, to me, looked a glorious shade of honey brown. She got a kick out of making fun of my so-called "addiction" to solariums, which developed during the icy depths of winter in Melbourne. I'd been working down there on an editing gig, just to tide me over until my preferred career option of Famous Author rolled around.

***

I'd been working at an office in Lonsdale Street, just down the road from *The Age* newsroom. I'd once applied unsuccessfully for a journalist position there and now, through a cruel twist of fate, walked past it every morning to a far less glamorous job. It worked like this: former employees with wages disputes or unfair dismissal claims slugged it out with their former bosses in the Industrial Relations Court in front of a Commissioner wearing twenty-four carat gold cufflinks and a silk tie. A court monitor recorded the case, then a typist transcribed the audio and gave it to me, the Transcript Editor. I was basically the quality control officer, tidying the document up so the words were fit to be sold back to the people who spoke them. A quick line edit, spell check and format. Easy, in theory. But in reality, an accent, a slur, a cold or a misplaced microphone during the original courtroom recording could mean a hundred-odd pages of pain for me. The typists (paid for speed, not accuracy) would leave blank spaces in the transcript when they couldn't make out what was said. The gaps, which were represented by the three dots of an ellipsis, were called 'indistincts', and it was my job to fill them … many of them. Eyes closed. Headphones on. Play. Listen. Stop. Rewind. Play. Listen. Stop. Rewind. Play. Listen. Stop. Rewind. Play. Listen. Stop. Sometimes, if you listened long and hard enough, the words would take shape, the way forms materialise before your eyes the longer you spend in the darkness. "In Michael Jackson" eventually morphed into "immunisation". The phrase, "You won, you're wrong!" (replayed seven times) coalesced into "You're on your own." But most of the time, I was flailing in the inky depths, chasing shapeshifting silhouettes. Drowning in an ocean of words that weren't there, I grew to accept that were some spaces I just couldn't fill.

Unfortunately for me, as the Transcript Editor, I was the last link in the chain. On the phone with customers complaining about mistakes, misquotes, or transcripts riddled with holes, I'd zone out. I'd bide my time until lunch, when I'd try to stay warm in the bitter Melbourne cold, avoiding shadows cast by skyscrapers that shrouded the city in darkness on even the brightest of days. I took an unusual interest in an oasis in the foyer, where someone had the foresight, long ago, to plant palm trees whose fronds reached high into the open air above the atrium. In bright sunlight, the palms shimmered and gleamed like a brumby's mane, tousled by the breeze on windy days. Diamonds cascaded down the ribbed satin leaves when it rained, sparkling droplets shattering on the lacy arms of tree ferns or beading on the evergreen carpet of Baby's Tears beneath. An earthly paradise behind a humble glass façade directly opposite The Gentlemen's Club—one of many strip joints at the seedy end of town.

***

One day, the General Manager came past for a chat, joking about how fortuitous it was that I, a writer (he'd remembered that from the interview—Employee Small Talk 101) had been helpfully seated at the window overlooking the Gentlemen's Club—able to see the comings and goings of the, 'Ahem, employees and clients [insert good-natured chuckle]

… hope you're not spending too much time making up stories about the ladies in there when you're supposed to be working—might be a book in it, eh?'

Strangely enough, not long after this exchange, my line manager moved my desk so I faced a windowless wall instead. There, I could only tell what time of day it was, or what the weather was like, via an oblong five-inch glass strip at the end of the room, through which all that was visible were people's passing feet.

And as beautiful as it was, I came to see the oasis in the foyer as a gigantic terrarium—an enormous, untouchable monument to the world outside—with me shrunk down to little more than a lifeless porcelain ornament within it.

**

In Melbourne, I lived in a freezing, rundown house on the outskirts of town with a lab technician who worked for the Defence Department. When we first met, I thought we complemented each other: Yin and Yang. Artist and Scientist. He used to laugh at my jokes about how one day he might come up with a Love Potion and weaponise it. 'A love pandemic, ha! ha!' Over time, though, he grew cold and distant, unknowable as the Sphinx, leonine face glued to his computer screen, watching online porn late into the night and playing violent video games for hours on end—retreating into the darkened study straight from work.

By then, I looked forward to his regular top-secret work trips to who-knows-where until who-knows-when (it was all "Classified"—in the national interest and all that). Blissfully alone, I'd wander the grass trails of Thompson Reserve with his dog, Xena the Warrior Princess, to a ford in the river known as Rocks Across. There, on a boulder rising from the gurgling waters of the Maribyrnong, I'd pretend I was on the bow of a great ship cutting through the ocean—carrying me far away from that western suburbs wasteland.

**

One Sunday morning, the Scientist and I decided to try "getting back to nature" as an alternative to our usual "hair of the dog" approach to hangovers. I drenched my pasty white skin in fake tan, packed my togs and we headed for the nearest waterhole, bracing ourselves for the plunge into ice-cold water. But it turned out swimming was forbidden at Sugarloaf Dam, where water filtered up through the Maroondah Aqueduct and the Yarra River, feeding into Melbourne's drinking water supply. The waterhole was crystal clear and lifeless; a chill wind cross-hatching the surface. Starbursts of clay particles drifted out from the bank with every gentle thud of the wavelets on the shore. There wasn't even room for sunbaking: just a bank of stunted dead grass shoots right up to the water's edge, minute spiderwebs shimmering through them like a vast, silken fishing net. My shadow, lengthened like a giant in the afternoon sun, loomed before me in the rippling mirror and it hit me, clear and stark: my own well had run dry.

I said to the Scientist, 'I don't want to work in a mind, body and soul-destroying job.'

'No one does. They still do it.'

'I know. I've tried. I can't do it anymore.'

'Well, what do you want to do?'

'I want to tell my story, not someone else's.'

'Well, why aren't you writing?'

Silence. Adrift in an ocean of other people's words … my own were getting lost somewhere in the depths.

'Are you going to tell me I don't understand the creative process?'

A jet plane glided silently through the sky, high above us.

'You're not a creative person.'

***

Okay, so maybe it was one too many Melbourne winters spent living in a fibro house with a single bar heater. Or maybe it was working in a windowless pit from morning until night with daylight eclipsed by a forest of skyscrapers. Whatever. The point is, I'd started craving sunlight in a serious way. I'd gasp when I caught sight of my ghostly white face in windows and bathroom mirrors: some days I even looked blue. It was probably a deficiency in more than sunlight but I started to seriously contemplate (when I was drunk at least) how I could find the money to buy a rooftop verandah (nothing else, only the verandah) that was for sale in a real estate window in Lonsdale Street—just so I could catch some sun on my forty-five minute lunch break.

Then one day, en-route for my twice-daily caffeine fix, I found a new addiction: artificial sunlight. A dollar a minute seemed cheap to me, so I ignored the small-print warnings about skin cancer and braved the initial weeks dealing with sunburn and peeling, because those precious eight minutes in the solarium every second day truly thawed me out. Stripped naked, slathered in tan accelerant, I'd lie prone in a pod that closed on me like a coffin, encircled by what I now know are deadly UV rays. But I'd emerge renewed. Strangers commented on my "good colour" and the General Manager even asked if I'd been "getting some sun".

My burnished gold armour took the edge off the cold—bolstered me for my daily procession across the concrete flyover next to the stadium at Docklands, down past Spencer Street, watching women in business suits and high-heeled shoes mincing over tram lines (I couldn't fathom how they didn't trip and catch the tiny ends of their stilettos). Holding my breath at the stench of urine near the alley bearing an antique sign: *Commit No Nuisance*—I was surprised no-one had souvenired it yet. Past the quaint sandstone church where in the dead of winter once I saw a single yellow daffodil bloom, and the world slowed to a snail's pace one morning as wedding bells sounded and a bride swept past me into the gardens there.

My second skin seemed bulletproof—until one day, while walking to work through air so cold my lips couldn't form words to thank the cashier, I found myself buying a black balaclava at an army disposals shop. But I couldn't put it on. Thought it would worry people. I threw the balaclava in the nearest bin and continued along Lonsdale Street, my bronzed face a frozen mask.

Next thing I knew, I was sobbing in the work toilet; not wanting the job, the Scientist, the city—any of it, any more. Tears streamed down my cheeks like rain on the palms in my beloved atrium. I pictured myself crawling on all fours among the lush green groundcover—dodging velvet moss and maidenhair ferns—like the poet Mary Oliver did, then writing about it, to "see the world from the level of the grasses ... under the swirling rickrack of the trees". She called it "Staying Alive". I understood.

A psychiatrist suggested I ask my manager to cut back my hours to part-time. My manager agreed, then sacked me soon after. It was almost funny: unfairly dismissed from a job dealing in unfair dismissals.

***

When the alcohol ran out at my retirement party, I rode the last train into Newcastle, strode through Honeysuckle and drank myself sober at the Seven Seas in Carrington. Daylight glowed gold over all the lost souls on Shipwreck Walk. Out on the horizon, whales heaved themselves from the depths in half-arcs, lightly, like little fish jumping.

I made my bed on silken grasses in the jagged shade of palm trees standing sentry by the harbour. Towering above me, the bronzed figure of Destiny took flight towards the merchant ship *Mojo*, rust streaming down her sides like tears.

tu-kin-u-mil-li-ko

Bronwyn and Shane Frost

Wung-ngun-bai was tired, her yul-lo (soles) were sore. Her Konara (family) had u-wol-li-ko (walked) a long way this pur-re-ung (day). They had climbed up into the bul-kir-ra (mountain). The season was changing. She was not sure how Ngu-ra-ki (the wise one) knew, but he had told the konara (family) it was time wai-ta (to move).

When pun-nul (the sun) was high in the sky they had stopped near a creek for a drink of nga-po-i (fresh water) and something to eat. Tunkarn (mother) had put some mun-bon-kan (oysters) that had been cooked in the koiyung (fireplace) into her kin-nun (bag) when they left the koiyong (camp) this morning. Wung-ngun-bai had eaten these but that was a long time ago now.

Pun-nul (the sun) was pil-la-to-ro (setting) behind the bul-kir-ra (the mountain) when Ngu-ra-ki (the wise one) kai-pul-li-ko (called out) that this was the place for the koiyong (camp). It wasn't long before ti-ri-ki (flames) were in the koi-yung (fireplace).

Bi-yung-bai (Father) threw a moane (kangaroo) into the tir-ri-ki (flames) to kim-mul-li-ko (cook). The ko-i-pul-li-ko (smell) made Wung-ngun-bai Kur-rur-ka (mouth) water. She was so ka-pri-ri (hungry).

When the ka-rai (meat of the kangaroo) was ready to eat, Bi-yung-bai (Father) moved the pim-pi (ashes) away and kin-bun-til-li-ko (cut) the ka-rai (meat of the kangaroo) with his kul-ling-ti-el-la (knife) to ngi-ra-ti-mul-li-ko (feed) the Konara (Family).

It wasn't long before Wung-ngun-bai felt kut-ta-wai-ko (satisfied with food) and she bir-ri-kil-li-ko (lay down). She could hear Nga-ro-nge-en (Old Woman) and Nga-rom-bai (Old Man) wit-til-li-ko (sing) as she drifted nga-ro-bo (to sleep).

It was early ngo-ro-kan (morning dawn) and Wung-ngun-bai could ko-i-pul-li-ko (smell) po-i-to (smoke) from the koi-yung (fireplace). Most of the Konara (family) were yel-la-wol-li-ko (sitting on the ground) and were wit-yel-li-ko (talking). Wung-ngun-bai kur-kul-li-ko (jumped up). She was excited to see what would happen today. She looked around at this new ke-kul (pleasant) koi-yong (camp). She didn't think she had been here before.

Ngu-ra-ki (the wise one) kai-pul-li-ko (called out) to the won-nai (children), 'Ka-ai (come here), I have stories wi-yel-li-ko (to talk).'

All the won-nai (children) ka-u-mul-li-ko (assembled). Ngu-ra-ki (the wise one) said, 'I will yu-til-li-ko (guide) you.' The won-nai (children) wir-ro-bul-li-ko (followed) him.

They came to a shelter in the rock. Ngu-ra-ki (The Wise One) told the children to yel-la-wol-li-ko (sit on the ground). Wung-ngun-bai na-kil-li-ko (observed) pictures drawn on the rock. Ngu-ra-ki (the wise one) wi-yel-li-ko (talked) and wit-til-li-ko (sang) stories about these pictures.

When he had finished, he mixed up ko-pur-ra (yellow ochre) and asked each won-nai (child) to ka-ai (come here) to the rock and place their mut-tur-ra (hand) there. Ngu-ra-ki (the wise one) bom-bil-li-ko (blew with his mouth) ko-pur-ra (yellow ochre), leaving the shapes of each mut-tur-ra (hand) on the wall.

Ngu-ra-ki (The Wise One) wi-yel-li-ko (told) the won-nai (children) this place was special and they had tu-kin-u-mil-li-ko (to take care) of it.

As the won-nai (children) grew, times changed for this Konara (Family) and they weren't always able to go to this special place with their won-nai (children) to tu-kin-u-mil-li-ko (take care) of it.

Red Fog

Abigayle Carmody

A quick, blinding glimpse through the curtains was enough to scorch my retinas. Nothing but white heat. Out there it was forty-two Celsius. Sun set 8:10 pm. Another ten hours of hell.

While I measured light, my husband was working in the desert where the blistering sun could be deadly. But he was too busy tracing silvery lines along ancient rocks to bother about the heat.

'Rocks as old as the earth itself,' he'd tell me each time he returned home from field trips. His skin would be covered in desert dust. His words would shoot rapid fire from his dry and cracked lips. It was a change from hearing about geological project plans and budget nightmares from head office. These days, he raved about fragments of diamonds in the oldest zircon crystals ever found. 'Over a billion years old! Imagine that,' he'd say.

I couldn't. What I wanted to imagine was the palette of this strange land and capture its colours. But it was only disazo brown I could see—dull and lightfast. Harsh hues for solid slabs of earth. A dome of sky that suffocated. The watercolour paper I'd brought with me from the city remained blank—like me.

***

Thalo crimson was the colour I turned when I ventured outside for food supplies. In the time it took to dash from the front door to the car, I was already covered in sweat. Through the windscreen, the earth shimmered ghostly. Silver white and gum laden—a filler. The melted lipstick I found in the bottom of my bag created a pool of French vermillion red—a vibrant, messy stain.

It was a short drive to the main street, with a view of nothingness at both ends. By the time I parked the car, I was suffering from a bad case of vertigo. I never thought I could experience such a thing on flat land.

The supermarket, more a general store with a few aisles, was pleasantly cool. In an attempt to hide the haunted face I saw in the mirror each morning, I kept my eyes downcast. My fish out of water look was instantly recognisable here. Locals don't miss a thing.

***

On our first evening at the one and only pub in town, my husband, Eli, mingled with the locals as though he'd known them all his life. I was eyed suspiciously in my too-smart gear—wearing heels for god's sake. I felt even more alien when Eli told everyone he'd somehow gathered around our table that I was a watercolourist. The locals regarded me with feigned interest. 'An artist? What sort of job was that?' I looked into my drink. Someone said, 'There's plenty to paint around here. Colours you don't see anywhere else.'

I saw only emptiness but mumbled some sort of half-hearted agreement. A woman named Dora offered to take me to some gorge for a swim. I smiled hard but had no intention. Besides, she was a complete stranger. *What if the car broke down and there was no reception? What if I swam in this gorge and got rolled by a crocodile?*

***

In the store, I took an inordinate amount of time deciding on one of the five shampoos on offer. My hair used to be normal but was now dry, bordering on damaged. I chose a product that promised miracles and flipped the bottle into my trolley where it rolled around amongst a packet of instant noodles and a tin of three-bean mix.

A few women were in the store pushing trollies containing supplies for one. Mostly older, perhaps with grown-up children now living in the city and left with their husbands working in the mines, or chipping away at rocks like Eli. I was the only woman there wearing impractical shoes, straps cutting into my heat-swollen feet.

In the tinned fish section, I spotted Dora. Broad shoulders, tanned leathery arms, salt and pepper hair that might have once known a style. Worried she'd offer to take me to swim with crocodiles, I executed a quick U-turn and hid in the frozen foods area. Leaning into its coolness, I was tempted to climb in the freezer and tuck myself among packets of peas. When the coast was clear, I headed to the cashier and tried to let her know I was in a hurry. Nobody was in a hurry here.

'Heard about the storm coming later this afternoon?' said the cashier. Name tag: 'Jackie.'

'Yeah,' I lied. 'Hope it'll pass over quickly.'

Jackie gave me a pitying look as if to let me know I didn't have a clue.

'Reckon there could be a dust storm.' She picked up my packets of double-choc Tim Tams. 'Need a cooler bag for these.'

'Oh, I forgot to bring it.'

Jackie pushed out her lips. I imagined her thinking: *Yeah, like you've got one.* Instead, Jackie silently put the chocolate biscuits and several packets of jelly beans into my organic cotton carry bag. I had the urge to explain to Jackie that the jelly beans were for keeping in a glass jar as a colour display. *Lollies for inspiration ... I am getting desperate.*

'Hubby's away, isn't he?' *Jesus, was that any of her business?* I didn't answer. Unfazed, Jackie continued. 'Storm won't be too much of a ripper but Dora'll text in case you want to head to the pub.'

'But she doesn't have my number.'

Another look from Jackie. Another rookie mistake. I remembered Eli had said something about working with Dora's brother and that everyone looked out for each other. But still.

***

Back in the car, the steering wheel nearly took a layer of skin off my hands. Mine was the only car without one of those silver shields covering the dash. As I made a beeline for home, holding the wheel with my fingertips, I made a note to get one. The sun was behind me. Six hours until it sunk into the Indian Ocean—miles from here. It was a long time to wait for small relief. When Eli was home, we'd venture outside at night and take in some fresh air, still soupy thick. We'd lie on the earth and look up at the stars. Him beside me, drinking in the wonder of the desert sky. I felt infinitesimal. Here, the night sky looked more like a mass of swirling galaxies shot out from the mouth of eternity.

***

While melted Tim Tams were resetting in the fridge, I took a cold shower. Then I put the air conditioner on full blast and got horizontal on the couch. Along with the air con, a three-speed fan was centimetres from my face. I watched some daytime TV for colour and movement: an upbeat Oprah. I thought about the thunderstorm that was supposed to be on its way. It filled me with a yearning for the smell of rain—to mix emerald with rich cobalt blue, greens and terre verte. Paint ferns and forests and layer the earth with deep brown pigments. Shape treed hills and cool blue rivers that slid through my memory. Faraway lands.

Anxiety clawed at my chest about the art I was supposed to be working on for an exhibition. In my proposal, I wrote about burnt skies, spinifex, and desert peas on a scarlet land. The gallery was waiting for me to send some images. I was just waiting.

***

I woke up with one arm dangled over the side of the couch and spittle on the edge of my mouth. I wasn't sure how long I'd been asleep. For a moment, I tried to forget where I was and imagined I was floating in a sweet breeze that wasn't just a fan blowing in my face.

The TV was still going. The last thing I vaguely remembered as I'd dozed off was watching *The Bold and the Beautiful*, wishing Hope wasn't so confused about Wyatt.

Then the announcement of the news with music that always sounded like the end of the world was nigh. The name of a place in the north-west was mentioned. It was a couple of beats before I realised it was where I lived. I sat up and peered at the image on TV: a swirling white shape hovering over a huge area the size of a planet, like creamy frosting on a marble cake. This town, in the east Pilbara positioned somewhere underneath it. I traced my eye north to the area Eli and his team were working, relieved to see it was outside the storm zone. The newsreader reeled off strong wind warnings of something or other knots and a possible dust storm. Nothing about rain. Glorious rain.

***

I was sucking on an ice cube when my phone pinged. A text from Dora: 'Storm on the way. Eli and team okay but out of reception. You can come to the pub. Everyone's here.' *Of course Eli was okay. Working in the vast desert was his dream. Painting it wasn't mine.*

I considered Dora's offer. It felt like an effort. I was in my underwear and sucking on an ice cube. *Why would I want to be with everyone?* I texted back: 'Hi Dora, thanks but should be okay.'

An immediate reply. 'Righto. Stuff wet towels around doors and windows.' That felt like an effort too.

I opened the curtains to see the shift in mood of the pending storm. Piled up on the horizon was a wall of thick charcoal clouds with layers of deep grey, mixed with chalk for pale tones. Earth a dull cappagh brown—barren except for the odd patch of sap green grasslands.

Leaning out the window, I felt static in the air, a sucking of energy, ready for release. I closed the window and made my way back to the couch. Overcome with drowsiness, I gave into the somniferous state that had enveloped me since arriving here.

***

My eyes snapped open to the sound of screaming outside. A haunting wail circled the house like a chorus of mourners had their open mouths pressed to the walls. The noise rose and fell, pitched and moaned. It rattled windows and found gaps to howl through.

Remembering Dora's advice, I dashed to the bathroom, ran water over some towels and pushed them under the doors. Sheets of blank paper stacked on the table had scattered across the floor. Doors bulged and threatened to come off their hinges. Dirt and sand spat through unseen crevices, landing on my skin like dancing ants.

I wished Eli were here. I picked up a rock from his collection on the shelf and turned it over in my palm—felt its warmth, its shape was like a tiny bone of the earth's soul. I held the rock tight as the wind howled and raged. It felt personal. I thought about Dora and the locals gathered at the pub and imagined them looking out at the storm—facing its power together.

Overcome with the urge to see the storm's fury, I stepped up to the window. My pulse quickened at the sight of an otherworldly force blocking out the sky. Hundreds of meters high, a billowing ochre creature rolled towards the town, swallowing up red and brown soil from the belly of the continent, its giant feet stepped across the land with terror and grace.

After weeks of claustrophobic stillness and squinting into thousand-watt brightness, I couldn't draw my gaze away from the thick red fog shrouding the air. A ripping sound on the tin roof snapped me out of my reverie and had me nose diving under the kitchen table—knocking over a glass of water along the way. A river of liquid snaked toward me, collecting rust-coloured particles in its path. A gust of wind made a sheet of paper fly like a bird and land in the stained water. Shades of ochre flowed across the page like an unfolding landscape. I stared into the image, drawn to its accidental beauty.

When the storm passed, I knew what to do. Cadmium orange and yellow. Intense violets would capture the hues of the twilight storm sky. To draw the earth in closer, I'd contrast shimmering light with raw sienna and burnt browns so that it tugged at the land.

Conversations with God at the Fernwood RSL

William Stanforth

Dad reckons the pokies have a way of telling you what you're worth. He said they speak on behalf of God or the universe. 'Why else do people pray or rub pendants when the reels spin? Why do they touch the screens as if reaching out to touch a religious icon?' He said this to me and my older brother, Liam, while driving from the chicken shop to his apartment. 'It's just like your grandma does with the statue of Jesus she keeps in her dining room. You know the one, you boys said it looked like Jared Leto.'

'Oh yeah,' said Liam. 'But that statue doesn't work.'

'How do you know?'

'Grandma let us touch it when George ran away.'

'Well,' said Dad. 'Maybe George found a better life somewhere else.'

'What's wrong with us?' I asked but Dad didn't hear me as he turned off the highway to his new place. Dad's new place was an apartment in a two-storey redbrick complex that smelt like cigarettes.

George was our chocolate-coloured Labrador who ran away when Dad moved out of our house, or when Mum kicked him out, which is what he'd say about it. We touched Grandma's statue and I prayed for our dog until I got dizzy and fell down. George never came home.

***

Liam and I sat in Dad's apartment and ate hot chips. All the while, Dad and his neighbour, Eric, stood on the balcony drinking beers and smoking Winnie Blues. When it got dark, Dad told us he was going to the Fernwood RSL and we weren't allowed to come with him. 'Eric's next door if anything goes wrong,' he said. 'Liam's in Year 6. You're both getting older—you'll be in high school soon—and you need to start taking care of each other.'

Liam's tall for his age and Dad reckons he'll be an athlete, like Dad almost was. 'Whereas you take after your mother,' he said to me not long ago. 'You're a bit sensitive.'

Dad left, and Liam and I cooked Maggi two-minute noodles because we were still hungry. I forgot to turn off the stove and a tea towel caught fire while we were playing GTA on Dad's TV. It set off the smoke alarm in his building and everyone had to evacuate.

Eric rushed in and threw water on the stove. There wasn't much damage when the smoke cleared. Still, the firemen showed up because they said they had to. And they weren't even mad at Liam or me, but they did yell at Dad when he got back from the RSL, which was weird because Dad wasn't there when it happened. He had nothing to do with the fire. Everyone's always giving my dad a hard time.

'They're just a bunch of angry, roided-up so-and-sos,' Dad said. 'They're dumb, meathead c-words who're desperate to be heroes,' he told us. But he didn't say 'so-and-sos' or 'c-words'—he said the actual swears. A year ago, those swears got Liam and me after-school detentions.

***

The next weekend, hours after Mum dropped us off, Liam and I had to go to the Fernwood RSL with Dad—because of the fire last week. Dad let us watch him while he spoke to God through the pokies. He moved from *Genghis Khan* to *Aztec Empire* and, finally, to *Panda Magic*. 'Major jackpot,' Dad said. 'I can sense it.'

Liam and I ran around the gaming room, playing hide-and-seek between the rows of pokies with their flashing lights and loud, bleeping noises. I hid in a corner, under a table that held Nescafé coffee in an urn and unused mugs. Though it wasn't Liam who found me—it was a barmaid with tired, wet eyes who seemed both angry and sad.

The barmaid led Liam and me to Dad, and yelled, 'Mick, you can't have these boys in here. Didn't you see the f-ing sign at the entrance?'

Dad took us to the other side of the RSL where a crowd of men were drinking and spilling beers and screaming at about ten different TVs stuck to the walls. Dad gave us two gold coins for the *Big Buck Hunter* arcade game and said about the angry-sad woman, 'Rich of her to act as a bastion of morality when she's working here and running the place. Needs to get off her f-ing high horse, I reckon. What a nosey, judgemental so-and-so.'

Liam said to him, 'Two dollars is only enough for one game.'

'Well,' said Dad. 'When it's over, just hold the guns and pretend you're still playing, okay? Especially if *she* walks past and sees you.'

Liam groaned. I laughed to myself, thinking of that woman riding a high horse. In my mind, it looked like a normal horse with really long legs.

Dad went back to the pokies.

Liam said to me, 'I get to play because I'm the oldest.' He then selected *Moose Adventure* and straight up killed two bulls and a cow. I pretended like I wanted to play, but I didn't want to kill anything, regardless of it being just a game with make-believe animals.

I was desperate to watch Dad win the jackpot on *Panda Magic*—desperate for him to speak to the universe and for God to tell him that he's worth something—even if Mum doesn't want to be with him anymore and even if the firemen yelled at him and called him a f-ing idiot when it was *my* fault the stovetop was left on and the tea towel caught fire.

When Liam finished killing video game animals with the orange plastic gun, we sat in the *Daytona USA* racing seats, pretending to play and talking about Dad.

'He won't win the jackpot,' said Liam.

'Why not?'

'Because no one wins. Those games are for losers—that's what Mum says.'

'They're not!' I accidentally yelled. At that moment, the screaming men and the TVs had suddenly gone quiet and everyone in the RSL heard me. I was glad to see the angry-sad woman rushing towards Liam and me because my eyes were also wet and I didn't want Liam to know I was holding back tears. The woman once again took us to Dad and yelled at him, despite it being *me* who'd made the commotion. Then she kicked all three of us out.

Dad wasn't mad at me when we got back to his place. But he did tell us to go to sleep and said we weren't allowed to play *GTA* until tomorrow. Dad went and lay on his bed in the dark and I could tell he was still awake for a long time because he wasn't snoring.

I cried silently in my sleeping bag because Dad never got a chance to win the *Panda Magic* jackpot and, more importantly, because he never got a chance to speak to God and for God to tell him he's worth something.

The next Friday, after school, Mum dropped us out in front of Dad's place. We ate sausage rolls and Dad and Eric had their longnecks and Winnie Blues. Later that night, Dad drove us to the Fernwood RSL, but this time he told us to stay in the Toyota. He said he was going in for a bit and that if we were well behaved we could get Macca's soft serves on the way home.

'I want a McFlurry,' said Liam.

'If I win the jackpot, you can have ten,' said Dad. Liam and I cheered. 'But you have to be quiet,' Dad continued. 'You have to hide, and if anyone sees you, just tell them I'm in the IGA and that I'll be back in thirty seconds.'

Dad left. For a long time, Liam and I played I-spy-with-my-little-eye in the Toyota. We spied the surrounding cars in the carpark of the Fernwood RSL, the nearby IGA, the streetlights, the bin and the rubbish on the ground next to it. Then we got sick of playing.

'He's not going to win,' Liam said again.

'How do you know?'

Liam shrugged. 'I don't wanna stay at Dad's anymore.'

'Why?'

'Because he makes us do this.'

'But he lets us play *GTA*. Mum doesn't.'

Liam shrugged once more.

'Why did Mum kick him out?'

'Mum didn't kick him out,' Liam said. 'He chose to leave.'

For hours, we sat in the car, and again, I tried to hold back tears. Thinking about George, our dog, still missing, and Dad leaving us—if that were true. Thinking about how God must have the power to fix these things if only we could work out how to speak to Him.

At 11:13 pm, I realised that I needed to pee. I held on, hoping Dad was about to return, but he didn't. Then, at 11:29 pm, busting, I went into the Fernwood RSL to use the loo—hiding from the angry-sad woman. Afterwards, near the entrance, I could see into the gaming room, where Dad was hunched over *Panda Magic*. He wasn't playing. He wasn't speaking to God or anyone. He was rubbing his eyes and drinking a beer in gulps.

Outside, a policeman walked away from the Toyota. When he was gone, I got in and asked Liam what happened.

'He saw me.'

'Why didn't you hide?'

'I did.'

'What did he say?'

'He asked what I was doing here. I said, "Waiting for Dad to get back from the IGA."'

'And?'

'The cop said the IGA's closed.'

'So now what?'

'Dunno.' Liam yawned. 'Did Dad say when he's coming back?'

I shook my head.

At midnight, Dad finally returned to the Toyota. Without looking at us, he said we could get soft serves but not McFlurrys. We turned onto the highway and, just as the Golden Arches appeared in the distance, the Toyota filled up with flashing blue-red light.

Dad's eyes widened. He started breathing loudly and swearing at himself. When he pulled over, the same cop from before came up to his window and asked him how much he'd had to drink. The cop then told Dad to get out of the car and walk with him.

I couldn't hear what they were saying but it sounded like the cop was furious because he was yelling and calling Dad names.

***

When Mum picked us up from the highway, she didn't say much to the cop or anything to Dad. She had a big coat over her PJs, dark bags under her eyes. Her face was frozen until she saw me and then her gaze softened. She drove us home and, once again, I thought of George missing. I wondered why Grandma kept the statue of Jared Leto if it doesn't do anything when you touch it. I thought about why Dad played the pokies if God isn't going to speak to him. Or worse, maybe God did speak to Dad and told Dad that he's worthless and that the universe will just take his money and destroy his family for no good reason.

Back at Mum's, Liam turned on the PlayStation when Mum went to bed.

'She's not asleep yet,' I told him.

'I know,' he said, with his eyes locked on the screen. Liam played GTA and straight away stole a cop car and drove around following the road rules. Mum came into the living room and sat on the couch and asked Liam what he was playing.

'It's a game where you're a policeman and you help the community.'

Mum smiled and sat there a long time. She watched us and the screen, watched my brother drive around in a little cop car stopping at all the stop lights and listening to the police radio.

When Mum fell asleep, curling sideways on the couch, Liam really started giving it to the tiny video game people—driving into pedestrians and attacking them with all kinds of weapons.

I lay on the carpet, thinking about Dad and George. Was it possible they never meant to run away from Mum, Liam and me? Perhaps they weren't looking for better lives somewhere else. They might just be lost— out there. And maybe one day they'll be found.

Princess Coup

Ellen Rodger

Melbourne Cup Day visit. A large, boisterous worker asks how old Mum is.

'She's got a great figure,' the worker says.

But Mum is skin and bones. She doesn't have a figure. How can you say that someone with dementia has a figure?

The worker has dressed Mum up for Melbourne Cup Day by tying a scarf into a hat. Mum looks so well. It's make-up, I realise. I tell Mum she looks beautiful, and she laughs.

'Do I look silly?' she says, uncertainly.

I take out my pocket mirror for her to look.

'I look nice,' she finally says.

'Your mother loves dancing, did you know that?' the worker says. 'Your mother is a wonderful dancer. Everyone here is so surprised that your mother is my favourite in the dementia unit because she hardly ever talks. True, I say to them, but she loves dancing. And have you seen your mother naked? She's got the prettiest body. Not an ounce of fat. Nothing ugly. But she needs some perfume. She's the only one who hasn't got perfume. Do you think you could buy your mum some perfume in the sales?'

The horse race starts. I look at Mum's ticket and point to the screen. 'That's your horse,' I say. 'Princess Coup.'

***

Mum falls asleep when dinner is served. Her sandwiches are cut into triangles, their peaks squashed beneath plastic wrap. The woman beside Mum sets herself the unhappy task of moving cubes of cheese from one plate to another. She then wraps the cubes in a serviette and secures it with her finger, keeping the fingers of her other hand crossed. *Antiques*

Roadshow is on TV. A woman lays out all the jewellery she's collected from rubbish tips to be assessed by experts.

***

My sister is waiting in the car park. We go inside. Mum's headband is visible above the back of the couch. When Mum sees us, she bounces in little steps across the room with her arms held out, as though she's carrying something dripping.

My sister unscrews an old-fashioned looking tin of Nivea. The cream is full of whipped white peaks. My sister pushes up Mum's sleeves and massages the cream into the backs of Mum's hands. Then, with a tiny pair of silver clippers, she trims Mum's fingernails.

The large, boisterous worker offers us a plate of biscuits and Mum turns her hand upside down, trying to remember how to pick things up. We take Mum to her room. A man in tracksuit pants is lying face down on her bed.

'Get out,' Mum screams, and the man leaves, laughing into his elbow.

Mum tries to assemble a story about the man, the details frightening. Lying in bed, the man this far away, her eyes open wide, not being able to move.

We guide Mum to the chair beside the window, and my sister applies a pink cream to the hairs on Mum's chin.

'Ooh,' Mum says. 'It's cutting me.'

'Is it worth it?' I ask my sister.

'It's for the best,' my sister says.

***

I stay overnight at my father's. He gives me a parcel of Mum's books, her dry shampoo, and her hair conditioner. In the middle of the night I hear noises, as though someone is out in the driveway. In the morning, the door to Mum's study is inexplicably closed.

'My husband, my husband,' Mum says when we visit, but my father focuses on the other women there, eager to assist them in his impotence with the one he loves. The chairs in the communal room all face the same way, as though connection between residents is discouraged. Music is playing. "It's a Long Way to Tipperary".

The large, boisterous worker announces Happy Hour and at first I think she's joking.

'So there'll be drinking and smoking?' I ask.

Then I see that the tea trolley is laden with wine and beer.

My father helps himself to a drink and tries to explain to Mum the difference between yesterday, today, and tomorrow. He tells her he had bruschetta for lunch. He says he doesn't know how often to change the bed sheets. He tries to explain to her the purpose of all five switches on the wall. Mum keeps getting up and opening the door to the chapel.

Back in Mum's room, someone has stuffed a doll down her toilet.

**

Travelling out on the train in the late afternoon, the chocolate frogs I brought for Mum soften in my hand. In the communal room a volunteer entertainer, a very old man in a black suit and bow tie, is playing songs from the 1940s on a cassette player. He dances in the centre of the room with his arms posed as though he's holding a partner.

Mum and I get up and dance. We do the Hokey Pokey together. It's the first time in ages I've felt comfortable dancing. I laugh, and because Mum is so fragile, the force of my breath startles her, as though I've blown smoke directly into her face.

**

'I've been cleaning out your mother's notebooks,' my father says. 'I found another stash that she'd barely written in. And not just any old notebooks for your mother. Only the best, at twenty bucks a pop if I remember right.'

He is wearing a faded green cap with mesh vents. A Band-Aid near his ear merges perfectly with the colour of his skin. We are shopping at Mum's favourite department store. Once, she tried to buy six pairs of the same blue sandals in one go, then couldn't remember how to sign her name at the cash register. My father was summoned. Her credit card was confiscated.

In women's fashion, I pick up a scarf from a display table and try it on. Navy blue, with tiny red and yellow flowers, it makes me look healthy for the first time in ages. The fabric is warm and feels lived in. I search for the price tag but can't find it. I want this scarf no matter how much it costs.

Then a woman starts shouting at me. She says it's her scarf and that she left it on the display table while she was trying something on. It was her mother's scarf. She's had it for twenty years. The woman asks, what have I done to her nerves? I give back the scarf.

We forget to buy perfume.

***

I catch the train to the beach and sit in the shade of a headland. A pool with faded stencilled numbers churns in water from the ocean. An old woman in a bright yellow bikini carries goggles and snorkel to the shore, her tanned skin compressed in wrinkles.

The old woman swims out into the waves and slowly circumnavigates the pool. I can see the pink of her heels kicking up through the water. When she emerges, she walks along the promenade to the cold water shower. A young man pushing a stroller observes her with the intense attention she deserves.

I forget to buy a train ticket home and start crying when the transport officer pulls out his fine pad. 'My mother is sick,' I tell him, and he puts away his pen and gives me tips on how to calm down. After he leaves and I have stopped crying, I worry that he will come back into the carriage and think I was faking.

***

In the cosmetics section of Mum's favourite department store there is a new kind of perfume, slender glass vials of warm yellow aromatherapy oil with a ball bearing at one end to roll over your pulse points. Jetlag, Energy, and Sleep are fully stocked, but there are no vials left of Stress.

The sales assistant shows me a different range of perfumes as she tells me about the freak accident she had when she was a girl. She walks her fingertips across the glass cabinet to demonstrate what happened at the pedestrian crossing.

'And thank the Lord it wasn't worse,' she says. 'Because not a single person gave me anything for all the pain and suffering I went through.'

I forget to buy perfume again.

***

The large, boisterous worker is playing the piano badly. She hasn't turned the TV down, as though her amateur skills don't entitle her to, and the residents sit looking blankly ahead, not attending to either the music or the TV.

'Sometimes I stand here at the door,' my father says. 'Before she even knows I'm here. I watch her sitting quietly and she seems so lonely in herself. Then when she notices me she jumps up from her chair and nearly kills herself, bumping into someone's walking stick or wheelchair.'

Mum is trying to understand one of her old books and has underlined words and made scribbled notes in the margins. The scribbled notes look like complex cartoon brains.

'The problem with the book is that it doesn't tell you anything,' she says. 'Because there's a man and who is he? He's just there and then he's gone. And there's a woman and then she's gone too.'

The large, boisterous worker offers me a chocolate crackle that she says Mum helped make. I wrap it up in tissues and put it in my bag. Mum is worried about getting crumbs on her jumper. The jumper isn't hers. I dance with a life-sized doll from the toy basket and sing along to "It's a Long Way to Tipperary". When I am leaving, the large, boisterous worker asks if I would like a lift to the train station. It is dusk and the trees seem coated in sawdust. The chocolate crackle crumbles in my bag.

I don't see the standing sign at the train station and it makes a dramatic bang when I walk into it. The hem of my jeans swabs the cut and fans blood across my sandal. Mum would appreciate my desire to fuss over a minor injury. Once she mistook red ink for blood and felt pain.

On the train home, a woman with one broken sandal is handling a clump of tangled jewellery. Something loosens and she pulls a silver ring from the mass. I watch as she announces that the ring is too small for her fingers. She holds it out to me as though for appraisal, then tries to push it onto my finger.

72

'No, no,' I say. 'Keep it for yourself. Or give it to someone you love. Give it to a little girl if it doesn't fit you.'

This seems to stir memories and the woman takes back the ring.

'The problem is that kids don't appreciate anything these days,' she says.

This settles something and the woman puts the ring in her bag.

***

Mum has forgotten how to turn her head and I have to stand in front of her to let her know I am here. When she sees me, she jumps up from the chair, strangely nimble. Her hugs have become their opposite, little pushes away and the accidental intimacy of her hand on my breast.

Mum steers me conspiratorially towards the dining table. Then she looks for something behind a wall hanging made of felt and broken earrings. We walk past bathing stations and laundries, then sit in a sunny courtyard with a highway on the other side.

I pick flowers and ferns from the garden and place them in Mum's lap. The bunch haphazardly forms the shape of a butterfly.

I can never leave cleverly. I always turn back to look and Mum is always watching me and waving dismissively, as though I am the demented one.

I forgot to buy perfume.

An Outing for an Introvert

Meighan Williams

Red flags hoisted all around as I perched awkwardly on a hideous moth-eaten sofa in the musty waiting room. It looked as though the owner had procured the couch straight from the set of *The Brady Bunch*. The springs were audible and protruding from the deflated, seventies-patterned cushions.

A Chihuahua, so ancient he could have been born on the sofa during its heyday, hobbled over and strained upwards on arthritic hind, desperate for attention. The presence of a dog within the purportedly clinical setting notwithstanding, I gave in to his demands and reached down for a pat. My effort was met with a punishing chomp as I became embroiled in an unexpected tug of war between flesh and fangs. Thankfully he was missing several, and I managed to shake him free, along with a few drops of my blood. He scuttled off down the hall. *Ouch! Little turd!* I was nursing my wound as she finally sauntered in.

'Right, 2 pm. Gift voucher. That you … Gina?' The woman's tone was flat as she scrutinised her clipboard, pausing before pronouncing my name as though it rhymed with a female body part.

'Yes,' I gulped, attempting to swallow my anxiety. *It's pronounced Geena, you fuckwit.* 'That would be me.'

'You shouldn't try to pat him.' She eyeballed my bleeding finger but made no offer of First Aid. 'He's blind and doesn't take kindly.' *I could have done with that advice two minutes ago. Some welcoming committee.* 'Right, come on through.' I followed her down the dim hallway, narrowly avoiding another run-in with "Cujo."

Julie had given me the voucher, despite knowing damn well my disposition, and had promised me that Cynthia was not only 'absolutely lovely' but also the best therapist around. I'd never heard of Mystic Massage, but Julie had raved about it. They didn't seem to have any sort of online presence, so I had gone in as blind as the old dog that now scratched and whined at the treatment room door.

She asked me why I was here. *Because I have a free voucher.* 'Because my shoulders are tight.' She asked if I do any exercise. *Does lifting a pint count?* 'A walk on the weekends.' She asked if I had ever had a professional massage before. *No, and it doesn't look like I'm ever going to at this rate.* 'Not really, just from my partner.'

Cynthia ordered me to strip down to my underpants and lie face down on the uncovered massage table. She handed me a tattered sheet ripe with the stench of mildew and told me to use it to cover myself, then stepped out of the room for what felt like ten whole minutes. *Wow, this is a great way to eat into my time. Does she do this with her paying customers?* I could tell she'd just wiped down the massage table, as it was still wet, and I worried that it might flare my eczema. *Great, it's only a hundred degrees in here. I'm going to sweat like a whore in church.*

The plinth had an odd curvature, and lying there prone, I was reminiscent of the time Julie had coaxed me into going to yoga class with her, and the discomfort that snake pose had caused.

When the masseuse finally re-entered, she didn't say a word, just pressed play on a disco-era cassette player. The air hummed with the unique, phlegmy falsetto of James Blunt. *How does she have this on tape?* My gut churned at the sound of his voice, but I kept it to myself. I didn't want to bother her.

As she edged past the table, I could smell her sweaty crotch; although that wasn't the word I held in mind for it. *Gina.* I stifled a laugh with a fake cough. It wasn't very convincing. I began mouth-breathing in a vain attempt to quash the musky odour, but this only served to increase my distress as I pictured the scent molecules planting themselves on my tongue and began to feel as though I was eating them. Thankfully, she shocked me out of this dilemma by thrusting a pair of aromatic bottles under my nose via the face hole in the bed.

'Which one do you prefer?' she posed, and switched back and forth between two woody options that were indistinguishable to me.

'Um, the first one?' A rising inflection betrayed the insecurity of my choice.

'No,' she decided without hesitation. 'The patchouli is more you.' *Then why the hell did you bother to ask me?* I let it slide. After all, I couldn't tell them apart anyway and she's the expert, right?

She poured the chilly lubricant directly onto my back and I shuddered before easing into its frigid relief. My front was already perspiring, and I had adhered to the coriaceous surface like a fly to the web. Without warning nor warm-up, her elbow jabbed me in the scapula and I let out a yelp.

'Should have warned you, sorry. Remedial hurts.'

'Okay,' I voiced feebly, quavering. *I booked in for relaxation, you dopey cow!* I quietly seethed but I didn't speak up.

This wasn't how it was supposed to be. 'There's no such thing as a bad massage,' Julie had assured me. *Why do I continue to take her word on things?*

I strained, guarding tender muscles; I did my best not to verbalise my cringes and winces. A few slipped out unintentionally but were met, if anything, by an increase in the pressure. This woman is a bloody sadist! Julie must be a glutton for punishment.

Having thankfully reached the end of the so-called treatment, that I can only imagine was originally intended as a CIA torture method, Cynthia abruptly stopped and walked out. She must have realised how weird this seemed as she quickly poked her head back in and announced that I could get dressed. I was slipperier than an oil wrestler and she hadn't even attempted to wipe me down.

I peeled myself off the table, feeling my back click in numerous places as I did so. *This can't be right.* She came back in too early and I was caught full frontal. *Could this get any worse?* She didn't even apologise as she turned and left, letting out an 'Oops!' on the way. *Thanks, Cynthia. For the worst experience of my life.* I paused and considered, for comparison, the night I had lost my virginity. The ungainly floundering, the flash of searing pain, and the fetor of Chiko rolls and VB. *Yep, this was worse.* At least Barry Benson had been gracious and possessed some degree of personal hygiene.

I collected my bag and shuffled out to the front desk where Cynthia was tapping away on a relic Apple Mac computer. 'When would you like to book in with me next?'

When Hell freezes over. 'I'm good for next Tuesday.' *Damn my mouth! Why am I such a spineless people pleaser? It's fine, I just won't show up.*

'We have a fifty percent cancellation fee,' she announced unnervingly.

'That's okay,' I simpered. *A small price to pay to end this uncomfortable interaction.*

A marginally older and affable woman emerged from one of the other rooms and addressed my masseuse. 'Thanks for covering for me Darlene, the RACQ took forever to arrive.'

'No worries, Cynthia.' She was still entering my next appointment into the system as the dog barked excitedly at her human's reappearance.

My heart skipped at the mention of her name, and I felt completely hoodwinked. *Tell her it was horrendous. Ask for your voucher back. And cancel that appointment before you end up out of pocket. Or worse, back on Torquemada's rack.*

'And how was it, sweetheart?' the real Cynthia kindly inquired.

'Fantastic!' I lied, detesting myself. I caught a smirk on the imposter's normally stern visage.

'Perfect. Darlene will see you next week then!'

'Can't wait,' I gritted, as I turned and hit my head on the inward-opening door in my eagerness to escape. *How could my day get any worse?*

The Worst Thing

Melissa Forge

Olli imagined it was going to be like a morbid gender reveal. The oncologist would pop a balloon, which would shower the room in confetti that was coloured to match a particular type of cancer. Pop! Teal. 'Congratulations, you have ovarian cancer!' Pop! Pink. 'What a cute little mass in the tit you have!' *What colour is allocated to bowel cancer?* Olli mused. *Brown? No. No marketing team on earth could make anything with the word "bowel" in it appealing.*

In lieu of confetti, Olli found herself staring at a scan with a large white mass in a place that a large white mass should not be.

'Please let that be where you ran out of ink,' Olli joked to the oncologist, unsure of why she felt so compelled to put him at ease. *What a horrible job,* she thought. *Having to come into work each day to tell an endless parade of people that they're stuffed.*

Olli couldn't focus on the words coming out of the oncologist's mouth. Her mind swirled, thinking about how she ended up in this tired and poorly lit consulting room. In the space of seven days, the future Olli had imagined for herself had swung from one of limitless potential to a cliff dive into the unknown.

Olli had moved to the city for the university. But the real drawcard was the independence that only bustling populations can provide. When you're the only gay in the village, small towns have a way of making you feel like a Markle at a Windsor family Christmas. However, Olli had not factored in the different kinds of independence. The moving-through-the-world-no-one-giving-a-toss-who-you-are-independence was what she craved. But she hadn't considered the reality of financial independence. No longer having all of her living expenses covered by the Bank of Mum and Dad had come as a shock. Olli was also about to turn twenty-one and be cut off from the family's private health insurance. Hence the rush to fix whatever was causing her lower back pain before she had to start paying for appointments herself. Olli had figured it was from the long hours hunched over her laptop in a chair sustainably sourced from hard rubbish.

A run of physio and osteopath appointments failed to find the source of the pain, so she was sent for an X-ray. A tumour compressing the disc above her L3 vertebrae had not been on her bingo card. Preliminary tests revealed it to be a secondary tumour, resulting in an urgent need to find the primary.

Every inch of her had now been scanned, screened, and scrutinised. She found herself in a tired and poorly lit consulting room because it was time to discuss results. Olli still couldn't comprehend the word soup spilling from the oncologist's mouth: stage four. Metastasised. Malignant. *No, no, no, this can't possibly be. There must have been a mix up with the results. Bowel cancer is for old people.* Olli's expression was in sharp contrast to the emotional chaos within.

The oncologist switched to support mode. 'Is there someone to pick you up? No? Would you like us to call someone for you?'

More words. None of them cut though the swirl. There was no one here for Olli because she had told no one this was happening. She had wanted to fully comprehend what was going on herself before having to explain it to anyone else. It was hard enough trying to keep her own anxiety in check, let alone having to calm a hyper-concerned mother who would have automatically jumped to planning a funeral before an official diagnosis was made. Olli realised that while she had been anxiously awaiting the results, deep down she had never really believed this is what they would reveal.

Cancer. She couldn't even bring herself to say the fucking word. Cancer was not supposed to happen to people like her. She immediately chastised herself. *It's not supposed to happen to anyone, so why should I be exempt from a few mutated cells going rogue?* But cancer wasn't supposed to happen to her because she was young and had plans.

The consult ended. Olli couldn't recall the conclusion but now found herself standing in front of a receptionist while fumbling through her wallet for her Medicare card. 'Are you free on Friday for the next appointment? To discuss the treatment plan?'

Olli pulled out her phone to check the calendar. Tapping the screen to dismiss a low battery alert, she realised she wasn't free on Friday, courtesy of a university exam. Olli stifled an eye roll. *Like exams even matter anymore.* Olli caught herself, slightly ashamed of the nihilism that now coloured the plans she made before. *It is a diagnosis, not an automatic death sentence.* Olli knew how to work her way out of any problem, only she had never found herself facing one of this magnitude.

She decided to make herself free on Friday, certain that no study would be getting done between now and then anyway. Olli waited patiently for the receptionist to fill out the appointment card. The receptionist was a kindly woman who offered to call Olli a taxi—concerned about Olli's ability to navigate herself to the train station and home in her daze.

Olli politely declined the cab ride, even after weighing up the high likelihood of a full-blown public meltdown on the train. To Olli, having to make small talk with a stranger in a cab was a decidedly worse option. What was she supposed to say? She imagined climbing in and getting hit with the classic: 'So, how's your day been?'

'Fantastic! Just found out I've got stage four bowel cancer. You?'

It was close to peak hour and the anonymity of a crowded train was too appealing.

***

Olli arrived at the station, skipped down the escalator towards her platform, and merged with the herd of people moving themselves from point A to point B—each one caught up in the minutiae of their own lives and all too busy to spend time pitying a stranger.

Olli managed to nab a seat on the train despite the crush. Unable to get a clear view out the window and unwilling to stare down at her well-beaten sneakers any longer, Olli scanned the carriage for people she thought looked more miserable than she felt.

A man. Mid-fifties. Hair greying at the temples. Sharply dressed in an expensive suit. He stared down at the phone in his hand, jaw clenched and face glowing red. *Probably just lost a million bucks on the stock market,* Olli told herself. *Sure, it was probably his clients' money, not his own, so no biggie. But now he won't get his bonus and has to tell the missus when he gets home that their Lake Como trip is off. Devastating!*

A teenage girl. Long blond hair pulled back in a tight braid that draped over the shoulder of her private school blazer. Her hands fidgeting in her lap for a screen to scroll. *Principal must've discovered that TikTok burner account she was running that rated teachers in order of fuckability. Her shiny-new iPhone is now confiscated. Mortifying!*

Olli enjoyed this game and felt a degree of superiority as she sat in judgement of the imaginary problems of strangers. Creating a scale of things to be truly miserable about, she was confident she had them all beat.

'What is wrong with you?' A sharp voice snapped Olli out of her smugness. Concerned for a split second that her inner-monologue had been said out loud, Olli looked up to discover an elderly woman standing over her and poking an arthritis-gnarled finger in her direction. 'These seats are for the elderly and infirm, not lazy, young upstarts. Move!'

Olli glanced down and noticed her seat was coloured bright orange, which was a sharp contrast to the royal blue upholstery of the other seats. To her right, clear as day, a sticker advertised the space as priority seating. Olli stood up and shuffled her way down the crowded aisle, a rosy flush of embarrassment burning her cheeks.

The elderly woman wedged herself into the priority seat, unconcerned by who she whacked with her errant walking cane in the process. She glared at Olli, basking in the moral victory.

At what point would I qualify as 'infirm?' Olli asked herself. She looked like a fit and healthy twenty-year-old, but in reality, the ancient woman Olli just gave her seat to was now highly likely to outlive her. The enormity of that realisation hit, and Olli began to choke back tears as the train pulled mercifully into her station. She jockeyed towards the exit, desperate to avoid eye contact and to keep it all together. *No, not here, not now.* She paced briskly towards her apartment building. *Get home. Get inside. Then lose your shit.*

Olli entered her apartment building and made her way towards the lift only to find an "Out of Order" sign stuck against the silver doors. The building's property manager was useless at repairing anything with urgency. Olli began to ascend the four flights of fire stairs required to reach her apartment. The compressed disc sent a searing pain of protest down her back with each step.

"Level Four." Olli pushed open the heavy fire door and began to search her bag for her keys. The keys weren't in their usual pocket. She dug further, assuming they had slipped out and sunk to the bottom, buried like treasure in a silt of empty gum wrappers and loose tampons. Nothing. Olli's fingers couldn't feel the cool metal jumble of the keychain. Once outside her apartment, Olli tipped the contents of her bag out onto the ugly and retro-patterned carpet. Panicked, she knelt down and spread the mess on the floor even wider before realising the keys weren't in her bag. They were nestled safely in their usual home—a bowl on her kitchen counter, which was on the wrong side of the apartment door.

Olli had left in such a hurry, distracted by the upcoming appointment. Fearful of missing the train, she had slammed down a mug of cheap instant coffee and rushed out, pulling the automatically-locking door closed behind her.

Olli picked up her phone so the property manager, who was clearly not busy repairing the lift, could come and let her in. A black screen stared back at her. The phone's battery was completely dead. Exasperated, Olli hurled her phone down the hallway and watched the useless device skim across the carpet like a stone.

The emotions she had been trying so hard to bottle up now spilled free. Doubled over with her face in her hands, Olli's body heaved gently in time with the sobs. Slowly, the sobs began to morph into a hysterical laugh that belied the seriousness of her situation. Aware of the absurdity, Olli sat herself up and leant back against the impenetrable door. She closed her eyes as she sucked in a deep breath—an attempt to anchor herself to the present. *The worst thing that's ever happened to you is the worst thing that's ever happened to you, right?*

Olli wiped her eyes, still grinning. On any other day of her life, being locked out of her apartment and unable to contact anyone would have been the worst thing that had ever happened to her. Today, it was a distraction.

The Marshmallow Game

Susan McCreery

As soon as I finished high school, I faked my knowledge of silver service and scored a job at a fancy restaurant in Darlinghurst. I was too slow and I couldn't uncork a wine bottle or carry more than two plates at once, so I knew I wouldn't last. But the reason they fired me three days in, on the day I learned of my cousin Steve's death, was because I turned up pissed.

As a kid, I used to get sent to my cousins' a lot. One time they took me camping down south near a river. Janie and I were eleven, Steve seven. My uncle, Dad's brother, barely budged from his camp chair. Beside him was a cardboard box for his empties, and several times a day my aunt would traipse over to the campground's recycling bin, upend the box, and place it back by his side. Us three kids shared a pup tent. In the middle of the first night, I heard Steve whimpering and squirming about in his sleeping bag, then rustling through his things. *What a baby, wetting his bed,* I remembered thinking. I hated myself for thinking that now.

I heard they were recruiting at the pancake parlour next to the cinemas on George Street. So I went along, smiled heaps, and got the job because it wasn't silver service. All I had to do was try not to be too slow or too awkward and memorise the prices and shorthand (SS + APS + C = short stack + apricots + cream).

The other waiters weren't up themselves at all. They were kind and helpful and funny, especially Peter—actor, gay. Peter taught me how to carry *four* plates at once. Tina, the Greek, had been there the longest and worked mostly in the kitchen. She had a temper but when she was in a good mood she'd sing 'Like to Get to Know You Well' by Howard Jones in this divine and husky voice. Tina was short, stocky, and her streaked ponytail would swish from side to side as she sped from hotplate to fridge and back. Tina was so good at her job, worked so hard, and was so respected—I fell a bit in a crush. When I was told she was to train me on drinks, my heart tilted.

The first thing I heard when I arrived on drinks-training day was Tina singing Howard Jones in the kitchen. *What a relief.* Duty Manager that day was tall Andrew, who never shouted. On the cash register was the lovely Tess—opera singer.

Tina showed me where the dry stock was kept. Then I followed her into the cold room, where they stored the ice cream, milk, and cream. I didn't want to annoy Tina by asking too many questions, so I stayed quiet. Her feet, in black sandshoes, were tiny.

Tina showed me how to refill the cream-squirters, fizz them with gas, and how to create the perfect swirl on top of iced coffees and chocolates. She also showed me how to make spiders and milkshakes and how to angle the stainless-steel milk jug under the steam wand.

'Have a go,' she said.

I tried to keep my hand steady.

'Not bad.'

When it was slow, I was to restock and clean my station: charge the squirters, refill the syrups, and make sure enough marshmallows were on hand for the hot chocolates.

***

My aunt had brought along a jumbo packet of Pascall marshmallows to roast over the campfire. When we were threading the marshmallows onto sticks, my uncle barked a laugh and said to Steve: 'Those marshmallow balls are about the size of yours.' And when I started rubbing my eyes because of the campfire smoke, he said, 'Do you rub your eyes when you wake up in the morning?' I nodded. 'That's because you don't have balls to rub,' he said.

At dusk, the kangaroos arrived to nibble the grass. The big daddy roos would loll back, scratching their balls. I guessed that's what prompted my uncle to start making jokes about balls. My aunt didn't say much. Sometimes I saw her flinch when my uncle got really loud.

***

When Danny, who was on dishes, ducked in on his break, Tina went right up to him. She wrapped her arms around his waist and tipped her head back, saying, 'We going to bed after work?' I busied myself with wiping down the stainless-steel prep area.

There were two wide pockets stitched to the front of our striped aprons. One side was for an order pad and pen. I kept the other side for my little flask of vodka. I'd taken a slug in the bathroom before shift. When Tina returned to the kitchen, leaving me on my own, I took another.

***

Next evening, when my uncle was at the campground loo, Janie and I pinched a can of beer out of the esky and snuck down to the river. There were thousands of big, beautiful pebbles alongside the water—all round and smooth and different shades of grey. Reflected on the river's surface were the huge trees on the other side. It was late autumn; everything was glowing and the air was cool and wood-smoky. I wanted to hire a canoe for Janie and me to row downriver, but I remembered her warning: 'Don't ever ask for anything.'

The two of us sat giggling and chugging our beer on the bank. Before long, we were half-pissed. I sauntered over to where Steve was earnestly trying to skim pebbles across the water. Back and forth went his thin, pale hand.

'Run and get us another can of Tooheys,' I said.

Steve shook his head, keeping his eyes on the water. 'I'll get in trouble.'

I drew closer. 'I know you wet your bed,' I whispered. 'I'll tell.'

He bolted.

***

Just as the cinemas began to empty, the sky outside darkened and the rain came pouring down. People started dashing back and forth across George Street. Headlights shone in the rain and lightning flashed. A queue started to form at the door and hug the side of the building under the awnings. I rechecked my stock and wiped the counter again. Tina appeared in front of me.

'Ready for the madness?'

I nodded and felt my neck go hot as I swayed and grabbed the bench. Tina didn't seem to notice. She inspected the two mugs of hot chocolate I'd put up and glanced at the marshmallows (one pink, one white) on the saucers. She gave me a nod and whisked the order away. I crouched down, unscrewed my flask and opened my throat. Like to get to know you well.

***

My aunt had taken the dinner dishes to the washing-up station. We were about to roast our marshmallows when my uncle told Steve to get ready for a game. Steve was to kneel in front of him with his mouth open. Without a word, Steve did as he was told. My uncle had the packet of marshmallows open on his lap. He held a pink one up like a dart. In it went, first go.

'No swallowing,' ordered my uncle.

Another one, white. Bullseye. By the fourth, Steve's mouth was full.

'Let's see how many will fit in your tiny gob.'

One by one, my uncle began to poke marshmallows into his son's mouth, pushing them in until Steve's cheeks were bulging and his tears ran. A long string of saliva swung down from my cousin's lower lip.

'Dad, stop.' Janie hadn't eaten her marshmallow and it was black and crusty like volcanic lava. Her father ignored her.

Steve's forehead was purple and a vein bulged on his temple. Janie raced over and brought her hand down hard on her brother's back and a pile of sweet mallow-mash issued from his mouth. Steve hugged his waist, coughing and crying over the mess. His dad leaned back and said, 'That'll teach you, you thieving little prick.'

***

Within an hour, my little station was hot and muggy. The floor was slimy with spilt milk and my shoes were soaked. The dockets kept coming and I scalded my wrist on the steam wand.

When Andrew dipped his head down to check on me, I was wiping my streaming eyes and nose with a paper napkin. *What a baby.* Andrew told me to take five, but I said I was okay. He asked if I was sure and said he could cover for me. I nodded and set two coffees on the counter.

When Andrew had gone, I crouched down to suck the dregs from my flask, then looked up to see Tina in front of me, her dark eyes unreadable.

'I've come for Cokes for me and Danny,' she said, moving to the dispenser. 'It's so fucking hot.'

Tina pressed the glasses to the lever and jabbed in a couple of straws. She then spun around and looked at me. My insides went to water.

'What the fuck are you doing?'

I stared at the floor. I could feel a big drip hanging off my nose and wiped it swiftly with the back of my hand.

'If Andrew finds out, you'll be history,' she said. 'And by the way, whatever's up with you, believe me, that's not going to fucking help.' She strode out.

May as well hand in my apron now.

***

By the time my aunt came back there was no sign of the dirty mass of marshmallow. Steve had been ordered to clean it up. I never said a word about sending him for the beer and never told him sorry even though I knew Janie was waiting for me to. After Dad moved out, I never got sent to my cousins' again.

Andrew ended up taking over on drinks, sending me out on the floor to clear plates.

'Cheer up,' said a customer. 'Can't be that bad.'

But it was that bad. I thought about the marshmallow game and about poor little Steve. I thought about my quiet aunt. I thought about Janie. We never spoke after that camping trip. I thought about the canoes and wondered whether they were still for hire. Maybe I could get in touch with Janie and we could go back to the river, to those beautiful pebbles and those great big trees. But if I was fired, I'd have no money for hiring canoes.

The rain had stopped and the rush was over. I worked the last fifteen minutes of my shift back at my station, cleaning up as best I could, all the while wondering, if I was fired, would they let me keep my apron and T-shirt? I stuck a pellet of gum in my mouth and shoved my empty flask down the bottom of the bin—under all the slops, coffee grains, and empty marshmallow packets.

Keeping my head down, I went to sign off, passing Tess. She smiled at me even though she was in the middle of cashing up. Then Andrew called me to the Duty Manager's nook in the corner. *Here we go,* I thought. I snuck a look at Tina, who was mixing up a big tub of pancake mix to be ready for the next rush. *She must have told him. Of course she had.*

Andrew was saying, 'Is that okay?'

'What?' I said.

'I'll put you on a couple of weekday shifts so you can get used to it. I shouldn't have rostered you on a Saturday.'

'I still have a job?' I said. I couldn't quite see what Andrew meant, like how I couldn't quite see out the fogged-up window behind him.

'You do.' Andrew flicked through his stock-order sheet. 'For now. Tina said you showed promise.'

I glanced towards the kitchen, but Tina wasn't about to look at me. She was singing. She clicked the lid onto the tub of mix and slung it into the fridge. She undid her apron and swung round to face Danny. Danny was all cleaned up and ready to go, waiting for her.

Warm Bodies

Stephanie Meegan Davies

The first thing Girl notices is the bodies swarming in various shapes, sizes, and shades outside the locked glass doors. The bodies are sweaty, shivering, and abuzz with the excitement. Water through glass.

The hot racing hearts of children clash with the cool Tasmanian-July breeze. One must feel the sun's blister on their face to understand how it is possible to be cold and sweaty simultaneously.

It's been a long and dry winter. Children walk the bank of the rivulet in single file. Back in the queue, bodies in different stages of undress wait in the sunshine looking like Komodo dragons basking on rocks.

By the time the staff at the YMCA pull the doors back, there are almost twenty people waiting—thongs, bare legs, and a twist of puffers on top. It's as if they had cut-out paper dolls whose bodies have been switched at random in some kind of sick joke. Bodies have been few and far between during the latest lockdown.

Girl inhales shallowly and opens the passenger-side door of the vintage Renault wagon. She is in her halter-neck bathers complete with polka dots. Both have seen better days.

Earlier, Girl and her mother waited in the car, chatting in fits and bursts.

'Can't anyone else follow instructions and wait in their cars?' her mother asks. 'People are useless.'

'I guess not,' Girl replies. *I'm one of those people, she thinks.*

They pass time listening to a soundtrack of ABC's Radio National. Curious strangers peer through their clear windscreen intermittently as if seeking to follow a leader.

Girl is not even her own leader. She is always a follower, except when she swims. Swimming is her superpower. Water has always been inside of her. Girl swam before she walked—frost misted her mermaid scales when she was a baby in a pool at the top of the world.

Without warning, the privilege of clean water for leisure was stripped away by a mysterious bug and the world shut down. Girl's heart is drying out with it.

In the beginning, the solitude is a dull ache like a Band-Aid. Technically, it's more like a sticky-ache until ripped off, when it burns. Girl is starting to forget people's faces.

Water is one of many things Girl's generation took for granted as they patterned their sheltered lives. Their generation, and the one's before and after, haven't lived through a World War or a pandemic until now. There's no famine or war in the golden country, though the truth is more nuanced. They think Live Aid was a concert, not a moment in time. The truth is that the poor inhabit an alternate reality without time to reflect on their surroundings. They wish only to bathe in a river free from dysentery and to live.

***

Girl and her mother slip around the glass panels with ease. Her mother is dressed head-to-toe in black like an installation. She strips poolside, as Girl flips her legs over the edge of her makeshift lane. The pool is back-to-front due to the Covid regulations. Lanes crisscross side-to-side in a way that is foreign but not entirely uncomfortable. Girl's lane is twenty meters max, possibly fifteen. She is guaranteed a lane for the first time in six dry months. It was pre-booked and somehow preordained. No walk-ins allowed.

Girl cannot swim in the shallow end and that throws her. The depth briefly choking her as she loses her footing on the edge. Girl prefers the shallows with the glint of tiles through musty blue-green. But a lane to oneself is a fantasy in this new world. She slips under the water's edge and temporarily forgets the black plague in her soul that mirrors the one on the outside. The water was inside of her all along. When it disappeared so rapidly, like a current rappelling over sleek boulders, a part of her dried out too.

Girl is concentrating so intensely that she doesn't notice her head slipping beneath the water. She's not worried. She swam before she walked.

Girl's eyes drift to the blue-green shallows now grey and distant. Her mind flows with the water to all the famous men lost at sea. It's always men, not women, who dominate the history books. She's certain more women have been lost in the ocean of history.

Harold Holt had a swimming pool named after him in Glen Iris. Olivia Newton-John's partner was lost at sea. Aaron Carter, Jim Morrison and Whitney all drowned in a bathtub. The sea has more than one way of swallowing a person. Though the facts swirl like the muggy grey water and envelop Girl until she cools. The water has a distant chill that permeates her pores.

Girl defies gravity and sinks down to the bottom of the pool, crossing her legs like a child. Her breath sends little bubbles to the surface. A part of her wants to stay there, protected beneath the surface from the troubled world.

***

The last thing Girl remembers is feeling safe at the bottom of the pool. She wakes with a splutter on her side, coughing up blood. The cold concrete has made her already cold bones ache even more. It takes a while for Girl to focus ahead.

After a while, Girl notices her mother standing over her, looking concerned. A lifeguard in slashes of red and yellow holds two fingers to Girl's neck, checking her pulse.

'She's going to be okay,' the lifeguard says.

Mother exhales, clearly relieved. 'The ambulance is on its way.'

None of this makes any sense to Girl. She is an excellent swimmer. Girl won her school swimming carnival in the backstroke—inter-schools too! Not to mention the medley relay with her classmates. Even though Girl is at university these days, her blue ribbons are still tacked to her noticeboard behind photos of her friends—a time capsule of sorts.

The air rushes back into Girl's lungs, temporarily winding her. It's hard to describe the feeling of fullness. If anything, it's the opposite of the tight feeling she's carried in her heart all year. The pain is exquisite, making her feel alive. Girl exhales deeply, letting go.

Events at the Synapse

Averil Bones

Red and yellow flowers drop down around me from the trees above. Pania, a dark skull with rubies for eyes tattooed between her clavicles, watches me struggle with the rented scooter.

'You right there?' she says, a wry smile across her face.

I'm flicking at the stand with my foot, trying to get it to snap back into position. I can't quite angle the bike far enough so the stand clears the gravel. 'Yeah, sure. I'll get it,' I say.

Pania waits. We both know I'm right. We've seen ourselves up the mast, struggling and terrified in heaving gales. We know each other's limits and this is pretty far from mine. If the worst comes to worst, I'll just drop the bike and hop away. We'll both laugh for a while and then I'll pick up the scooter and try again. But it doesn't come to that. I persevere until it clears, and we're both revving rented scooters in the island sun, muscles ripped and hardened from long hours and long days and long months at sea.

The take-off is surprisingly fast and I skid a little; unstable. I rush to follow the faded orange of Pania's singlet and pink bra strap into the sparse island traffic.

Charcoal burning, and something aromatic I cannot identify, makes the air a foreign place—interesting and exotic. I gulp down the syrupy smells of land after a long time at sea. As we pass, I see people barefoot under palm trees, some in thongs, ambling along the roadside, suddenly a pig laid out in the sun, and a glimpse into a desolate resort where bodies burned pink and red lay about a chlorine pool like fat flayed seals. Land feels good, but it's not the vast sandstone dry I know best.

The speed of the scooter turns the thick tropical air into a breeze against my face. I can feel the wind cool the sweaty clumps of hair at my temples and around the back of my neck.

Ahead, Pania stops at a crossing. I squeeze on the brake with my fingers. It's sensitive, and my arrival beside her is jerky and awkward. I can feel her watching me flail, amused. I'm a foreigner, a continental creature that does not so much belong here. 'Which way?' Pania yells.

While I'm thinking of the map, a beautiful rooster emerges. Plumes of feathers spill up and out of his tail and neck. The rooster pecks at leaf litter near an old street sign. I cannot make out the lettering, but I remember the map. Left, the long road past the swamp to the airstrip. Right, the winding way to the lagoon and village.

I point right. 'Let's go see the lagoon.'

Pania flashes a quick thumbs up, a wide smile across her face. She shoots off, her brown limbs wrapped around the bike.

***

The road is quiet now. It's just us and the high-pitched revving of our scooters through thick air and verdant forest. I like the feeling of motion, of the bike's centre moving under me as we round the rutted corners. I haven't moved so far and so fast for months.

The land drops away to the right and opens out into the view of a turquoise lagoon. It's dotted here and there with boats which show the rough fingerprints of tropical weather—worn and tattered. We come into a village that sits low down in a fold of the landscape, across the road from the lagoon.

Pania stops again in the shade, across the road from a group of men. I pull in behind her. The men look like a roadwork crew but they are deep in the grass behind a low stone wall. I can't properly see what they're doing.

'Look,' says Pania. 'They're digging.' I see the round shoulders of two men sweating in the sun, throwing shovelfuls of dirt up against the sky from the cover of grass. 'I guess it's for that.' Pania points to a roll of coloured straw matting laying in the shorter grass on the side of the road. The matting is tied neatly with flowers tucked into the string.

'What is it?' I ask, feeling a bead of sweat run down my neck.

Pania turns and looks at me, her black eyes amused. 'What do you think it is?' she says.

I look again. The shape of the thing laying in the sun. The tidy wrap. The careful weave of coloured matting. The flowers, gathered, bunched and carefully arranged. And the backdrop of the men digging in the long grass. I see its form. Its essence. I see the body-shape within it.

'Oh,' I say. No more words. I feel so unprepared. This vision is so much beyond me. My neat and tidy city life has left me without context or experience. Of this, a thing so common it happens a thousand times a day.

'Come on,' says Pania. 'Let's keep going.' I hear the click as the gear on her scooter engages. She saunters off smoothly, her liquid balance like a snake down a mountain. I jerk forward behind her.

***

In the main street of the village, there is water on the road. Shallow puddles shine like mercury in the sun. On the lagoon side, the houses are dilapidated and abandoned, although I see dogs and children playing amongst them. On the land side, marching up the steep slope, the houses look newer, squarer, and inhabited. By the road, a church—white walls cracked, spilling flowers of frangipani and hibiscus, and a black stone path with neatly cut grass.

We pull up outside a small shop, identifiable by the faded advertising painted across its façade. My braking is better but still lacks the easy smoothness of Pania's practiced glide.

It's quiet inside after the bang of the screen door behind us. Just the flicking of a fan blade and the sound of fridges running. Pania hands me a cold drink from one of the fridges, orange flavoured, and goes looking for someone to pay.

'Hello?' I hear her calling out down behind the shop.

'Yeah, yeah, coming,' a voice rings up the side path.

The shopkeeper comes in through the door which bangs again. A big man with big hands; a loose yellow singlet hanging down around his barrel chest with his nipples showing; baggy floral shorts and bare feet. In the dim light, his white teeth glow in his brown face.

'Oh, she's just gone around …' I point down the side where Pania had gone.

'Hey, girl,' he says. His brown eyes look me up and down. 'Where you from?'

'Oh, I've just gotten off a boat,' I say, taking a step back. 'We've been sailing.'

'Good weather?' he asks.

'Some,' I say, thinking of the moonlit sea. 'But not always.' The endless dead black nights of chaos and storms.

'Yep, sounds about right,' he says. 'You having a look around?'

'We are,' I say. 'It's nice to be on the ground for a while. What's this place called?'

'This is my shop,' he says. 'My father had it before me.'

There's a moment's silence.

'We saw this thing up the road,' I say.

'Yeah, what'd you see?'

'Well, they were digging, and there was someone laid out on the … well … near the road.'

'Oh yeah, we had the service this morning. No one much wanted to do the digging. Those boys'll be slow about it, probably be there all day.'

'Who was it?' I ask.

'Who died, you mean?' he says and I nod. 'It was one of the old girls. Noelani. She wasn't much liked really, but we gave her a send-off. I watched her beat up a dog once.'

'She beat up a dog?'

'Hell yeah. Better than taking it out on the kids, see. She was a good one for yelling.'

'Oh, so she had a family?'

He looks at me, as if I were a blind thing, to be pitied. 'We're all family here bro, no getting away from it.'

'So, she was your aunt or something?' Still dumb.

'Sure, whatever. My aunt Noelani.'

Pania comes back in, the screen door banging again behind her. The shopkeeper turns and looks her over—her wildness and strength. Pania's black eyes take him in too. I feel like they're seeing something about each other that I cannot see and cannot understand.

'Noelani?' she says.

'Hey girl,' the shopkeeper says. 'Where you from?'

'Pitcairn,' says Pania.

'For real?'

'For real. We've been sailing.'

'No kidding,' he says. 'Long way.'

A brief pause. 'You saw the digging up the road then?'

'Yeah, we saw. Up the road. You're laying someone down there for good?'

'Sure, she'll be laying down,' he says. 'Not sure it'll be for good though.'

I stop sipping from the flat orange drink. 'What do you mean?' I ask.

'Well, it's getting pretty swampy there with the sea coming in,' he says. 'We talked about putting her up the hill a bit, but she's by the church and she would've been pissed off any other way. We won't be burying them there much longer though.' We wait for him to continue, both drinking in the cool orange flavour.

'I guess we'll have to move them all up the hill someday,' he says. 'Or at least stop planting them there. High tide and they're all well under I'd say. Things are changing.'

Pania walks across to consider the ice-cream freezer. 'I guess it's all over the place,' she says. 'We saw the old houses on the lagoon.'

'Oh yeah, my poor heart. My old house, the one I grew up in. We used to have fruit trees, a beautiful sandy beach, and my boat right out the front. I live up the hill now.'

'You get big storms?' says Pania. The weather eye.

'Oh yeah, big ones roaring through. Sometimes, I just don't know where to go. Not like anywhere is that much safe. Up in the caves if it gets real bad ... but there's not much up there either.'

Pania hands me an ice-cream, then turns and gives the man some creased notes. He considers them, then fishes in his pocket for coins and counts out the change.

We all wander back outside, the screen door squeaking and banging a staccato as we go. Down the road, we can hear the men digging and talking, poking fun at each other and laughing—taking their time with the task. I think about the woman laying on the verge ...

'See, that down there?' The shopkeeper points across the road to a crumpled blue shack, its footings in a drift of sand and palm trees. Some of the trees tower over it while others are tilted, prone in front. 'That was my house. My father's house. Still hanging in there I guess.'

'Where are they now?' asks Pania. 'Your parents?'

He turns away from us and closes his eyes. He pushes back his wiry hair with a big hand. 'My parents?' he says, turning back. He points towards where the men are digging.

'In their swampy graves,' he says. 'Turns my stomach to think of them laying there with all that damp coming up beneath them. It turns my stomach. It used to be we all knew we'd end up laying there together, but not now.' He pauses, looking down. 'Turns my stomach to think of digging them up and moving them too.' He rubs his big hand across his forehead. 'I just hope they're resting easy,' he says. 'Not mad or anything.'

'I'm sure they'd understand,' I volunteer, hopefully and awkwardly out of place.

'Sure, are you? Not your blood that's lying in a swamp then. Sometimes, I think they're up and around at night. At me to move them. At me to do better for them. And the old people too. But if we move one, we're going to have to move them all. And the church. All up the hill.' I follow the line of his gaze up the steep slope stretching skywards above the village. 'It's a big job,' he sighs.

'Just start, and you'll get it done then,' says Pania forthrightly, ripping foil off her ice-cream.

'Oh yeah?' he laughs. 'You gonna help with the digging?'

A Guest at the Wedding

Russell Anderson

Shaun could empathise with Gough Whitlam who, that week, had been unceremoniously kicked out of government. Helen kicked Shaun out just as effectively. His latest drunken episode and another job lost was the final straw. Shaun left Brisbane by bus and ended up in Newcastle.

Shaun obtained a labouring job with contractors at the smelter. For the next six months he worked, drank, and wrote letters to Helen. The only reply he received was an envelope containing two drawings, which he presumed were from baby Christine. Helen probably hadn't sent them, her mother more likely. Instead of cheering him up, the drawings made Shaun more miserable and he went on a three-day binge.

Job lost at the smelter, Shaun picked up another with a concreting gang. The project was way up the Hunter Valley. The concreting bloke Shaun worked for was an Italian called Marco, a blond haired forty-odd-year-old, stocky with a pronounced gut. Marco would pick him up at 5 am in his station wagon then brought him back at 7 pm. The wagon also carried two other labourers, Charlie and Stef, who had been with Marco for years. Both were in their thirties and over 185 centimetres tall—dark hair, tanned faces and solid bodies. Some sort of Yugoslavs. They chatted in their language all the way there and back.

***

One day, Marco invited Shaun to his place. They were having a party to introduce a relative of his wife, Drusilla. Marco told Shaun that the arrangement was for Stef to marry the girl so she could become an Australian citizen.

'Marica is Drusilla's niece. They both come from a village in Slovenia. Charlie and Stef come from the very next village,' he said.

Thirty people packed the backyard. Marco was stationed at the brick barbeque, with a chequered apron and glass of wine. Charlie took Shaun and introduced him around. He stopped before a large, big-breasted, and raven-haired woman.

'Ah, so you are Shaun. Here, give me a kiss.'

Shaun felt moist lips planted on his and saw brown eyes looking straight into his.

Charlie laughed. 'This is the famous Drusilla!'

Famous for what? wondered Shaun.

Drusilla squeezed Shaun before releasing him. 'You are a handsome man, aren't you? Now, meet Marica, she speaks good English.'

This time Shaun received a peck on the cheek. His vision filled with dyed blonde hair and thick make-up spoiling what was otherwise a very pretty face.

'Hey, Shaun. You get some of this homemade wine. Not the cat's piss strength.' Marco proffered the flask and filled Shaun's glass.

Finding a spare chair near the large tree Shaun sat down and was happy to observe Marco performing at the barbeque. Drusilla scuttled backwards and forwards between the house and the party. Drusilla was always accompanied by two other large women and Marica. Marica cast a number of glances his way and smiled. Stef never left Marco's side, while Charlie mingled with all the others.

'He is like a son to me,' Marco said, his arm around Stef's shoulder as they sat down to the meal. 'And he's going to wed this beautiful girl and settle down forever.' With that Marco planted a kiss on Stef's cheek and forehead.

Shaun looked at Drusilla, who rolled her eyes and she shook her head, which he guessed was in either disbelief or disgust. Shaun observed that Drusilla was much younger than Marco.

The evening was enjoyable, made more so when Marco and some of his friends broke out into Italian opera. Everyone was relaxed after dinner. Shaun returned to the base of the tree and observed the others.

'You have a girl?' The voice came from behind him.

He stood and turned to face Marica. 'No, not really.'

'Oh, that's not right. You need someone.'

'I do alright on my own.'

'I don't like Stefan,' Marcia said, pouting and wrinkling her nose.

'Then why marry him?'

'There isn't anyone else, is there?'

Marica had moved closer to Shaun. She was quite small with her head tilted back to look into his eyes.

'I can't help.'

Voices called out from the house. Marica drifted back into the dark and headed around the wall towards the house.

***

The wedding was to be a civil affair and held in Marco's garden. Marco asked Shaun to help since Charlie would be busy looking after Stef. Shaun arrived to find the house in chaos. Drusilla was yelling at a group of women setting up tables and chairs. Marco was nowhere to be seen.

'He's gone to get fuel for the fire. You must help me in here.'

Shaun followed his boss' wife into the house and the main bedroom. Marica, his co-worker's bride-to-be, stood there in a lacy bra and skimpy panties. She smiled at Shaun unconcerned and unembarrassed.

'Shaun, you sit here and hold these clips while I do madam's hair. Now, don't move Marica, I don't want to hurt you. You'll get enough of that tonight.' Drusilla looked at Shaun.

'Stefan is huge. I thought I could take a bull. But him … he hurts you so. Marica you'll be so sore tomorrow.' Drusilla laughed and patted Marica on the bottom. Marica said nothing, just bit her lip and gave Shaun a forlorn look. Drusilla winked at Shaun.

'I shall have to find myself a new stallion, another beast. Are you a beast, a stallion, Shaun?'

Shaun smiled, shaking his head. 'I'm the gentle sort.'

'Poof! Who needs that? I have a husband for being gentle. Now Marica, get dressed, they'll be here soon. And Shaun, you can go now, thank you.'

***

Marica wore a headband of flowers; Stef was in a shiny blue suit. Stef towered over his bride. After a brief ceremony, the party got going. At one stage, Shaun remembered kissing Marica in the hallway.

'Where's Stef?'

'Servicing Drusilla one last time. I hope he wears himself out.'

***

The following day, Sunday, Drusilla and Marica called at Shaun's unit.

'I have brought this poor lost love one to you. I have to go, enjoy yourselves,' Drusilla said.

'Just hold me, please, nothing else,' Marcia said.

Shaun kissed Marcia and led her to the bed. Neither removed their clothes. They lay in each other's arms, kissing occasionally, before Marcia fell asleep, breathing softly.

***

Shaun and Marcia made love the following weekend and every weekend after. Shaun knew he did not love Marcia but welcomed the affection. As time went on, Marica became more urgent in her lovemaking crying out. 'Harder, harder. In me. Right in me. Oh, please!' And more in her own language. Shaun was certain that she wanted him … but now with Stef's equipment … it was beginning to turn him off.

***

Marco said they had a new job near Gulgong. Further to travel, but he knew of a short cut.

'No bloody drinking in the car. Okay you blokes?' Marco cranked his head backwards to further emphasise the message.

Shaun sat on the front bench seat next to him. In the back, Charlie and Stef had been giggling and leaning forward to dodge their boss' look in the rear-view mirror. They were on their way back and Marco was using the dirt road that ran along the Goulburn River as a shortcut. They were late and it was getting dark.

'Marco, you stupid ding. It's a special day. Marica's pregnant. Stef brought this almond brandy, you want some?'

'No, that homemade stuff will kill you.'

'Shaun, you try it.'

Shaun took a sip from the bottle; his breath sucked downwards as the strength of the alcohol burst through and burnt his gullet.

'B'Jesus! What is it?'

'Just almonds. Distilled,' said Charlie.

There was an almond flavour. It was pleasant once the burning sensation dissipated. Soon it was followed by a lightheaded feeling.

'Okay give Marco a sip. I might as well join the party.' Marco shifted his bulk, occupying two-thirds of the seat, and held out a hand. The bottle was placed in it. He drank deeply. He turned to Shaun.

'You should drink, Grappa. Get you used to this stuff.' Marco had another pull from the bottle with the same reaction.

'You keep that in the front, we've got another one back here,' said Stef.

Marco cradled the bottle between his legs, occasionally offering Shaun a sip. The light headedness increased and Shaun found himself nodding off, only to be jerked back to consciousness as the car veered around a bend. Both the men in the back were laughing uncontrollably. Marco was crooning in Italian. Sleep came to Shaun.

***

Bang! Shaun woke up as his head hit the car door, hard. He looked up. There was something wrong with the sky. He clung to the door grip as he felt the car tip over. Marco was trying to steer but his bulk was jammed up between the steering wheel and driver door. A glance towards the back and Shaun could see four legs sticking up. The car was sliding on its right-hand side. Shaun brought up his knees against Marco's backside. Their slide was slowing.

Suddenly, they dropped into the stone washout at the side of the road. Screeching sounds as metal was scraped and torn. A rock appeared through the glass above Marco's head, which bounced backwards. It was a large rock. They were still.

Shaun remained squashed between Marco and the door. He propped himself with one hand against the roof and relaxed his grip and reached for the door lever. Once he found it, Shaun pulled the lever down and pushed with his back. The door opened.

Shaun, crablike, worked his way backwards through the door. He rested a few seconds and perched on the side of the car. He leapt to the ground. The car's headlights were shining forward. No smell of petrol. Just almonds. He opened the rear door and peered into the tangle of arms and legs. 'You alright in there?'

Mutters in Slovene. A hand reached out. He grabbed it and pulled. More curses, then a scream and Charlie's bloodied face appeared. He worked his way out with Shaun's help. A bone protruded through his sock on one foot, his shoulder strangely hunched up. He sat beside the car and whimpered. Shaun could not reach far enough inside to get to Marco or Stef. Shaun tore his shirt to make makeshift bandages for Charlie's ankle and support for his shoulder. No sound came from within the car. A sore back seemed the only injury for Shaun. Then there were lights coming over the crest and down the road. He stood in the road, waving. The four-wheel drive pulled up.

'What's happened here?'

***

Shaun was kept in hospital for observation. The nurse broke the news that Marco had died from head injuries. Stef had critical internal injuries. Charlie would, in time, be fixed up.

'My man, my Marco, oh no, no.'

Shaun opened his eyes to Drusilla's tear-streaked face.

'Why him, Shaun? Why him? The very best man in the world.' Drusilla broke out into Slovene, wailing and grasping her blouse so hard he thought she would tear it off. Shaun said nothing, in fact, he found himself pulling the sheet up to cover more of his face. Marica's head appeared around the door—rivulets making their way through her makeup. She started to enter the room, then shook her head, sobbed, and retreated. Drusilla ceased her wailing.

'What am I gonna do, Shaun? Three children. I'm still young. What's gonna become of me?' He still could find no words. He had nothing to say. 'You sissy boy. You stupid Australian prick! Nothing wrong with you, is there?' And she gave a huge horse snort and went, stomp, stomp out of the ward.

Old Woman Crazy with the Snakes

Phillip Everett

The long, hot, and dry summer was forcing the snakes out from under logs and stray rusting sheets of corrugated iron. This was even during the daytime when kookaburras were perched in almost every tree. When hawks and eagles soared on the thin dry airs. It was sudden death for those venomous serpents. Thus, the snake numbers were thinned out dramatically, as the snakes moved in from the dried-up watercourses to the bores and homesteads to scavenge leaks from tanks and tubs. Times were hard, and hereabouts were much harder for serpents, because the Old Woman was on the prowl.

For maybe forty or fifty metres around her isolated farmhouse, Old Woman fastidiously removed every stick and twig. She placed it all in ever-growing piles, well away from her farm sheds and water tanks. Every blade of grass that still stood after the furnace blast of summer, was cut short and fed to her chooks. The wind whipped up clouds of dust that swirled and choked. It peppered her wide and shady verandas, carpeted roofs, and the leaves of plants and bushes nearby. Everything that grew near Old Woman's farmhouse was severely trimmed, so as to provide no opportunity for reptiles to lurk amidst leaves, grass or low-sprouting foliage.

Old Woman had been alone for all of fourteen years since her hubby, the kindly Alf (a casual and rather work-allergic individual), succumbed to the bite of a red-bellied black snake. It had been down underneath their bathtub, in the shade of a peppercorn tree. Alf had decided to freshen up a little from the heat.

Now, the exterior of that same tub bears the numerous peppering of shotgun pellets—Old Woman used up a whole box of twelve-gauge cartridges. She severely bruised and dislocated her shoulder in the dispatching of the lowly pest. It is said Old Woman didn't tend to her Alf until well after the serpent's life was terminated. It is still rumoured, that Alf's legs also bore numerous shotgun pellet wounds. Some (those who take unkindly to old age, infirmity, or the human race generally) say that Alf died, not of snake bite, nor of lack of immediate treatment, but died a lingering death of lead poisoning.

If you know anything of isolated bush communities, you'll know such persons may have a good tale to tell, but eventually find it hard to retain any drinking companions and their rounds of drinks at the local become rather flat and unrefreshing.

***

Old Woman sat bolt upright in her bed. She'd been dreaming of her girlhood. She swung her feet to the bare boards, and with a shuffling sleep-walk made her way along the hall to the front door. Old Woman took up a shotgun and moved out onto the veranda. She then shuffled to the very edge, closest to her orchard. Raising her gun and aiming it towards the orchard, Old Woman discharged both barrels in rapid succession. The recoil sending her staggering, reeling backwards, hard against the weathered boards of her house. In the crisp night chill she looked, wondering at the curling and curving wisps rising from the barrels of the gun. The smoke rising, not unlike that from candles on the altar at Alf's funeral. Eventually Old Woman turned indoors, propped the spent weapon habitually against the wall, and returned to bed.

She'd been dreaming of the orchards of her girlhood. Ancient pines and straggly fruit trees, desperate for a pruning. Back then, Old Woman wore a pinafore, broad-brimmed sunhat, and her stockings gathered grass seeds and burrs. In her dream she'd looked down, and a finger-thick, slate-black hissing snake, wriggled through the grasses between her feet. She stood rigid. Her chest thumping from her heart pounding within.

In bed, Old Woman's ears were full of her heart's pounding sounds. As her dreamed finger-thick snake disappeared into the grasses, young Old Woman looked away, the tension sighing out of her body. Slowly, as her heart quieted, she began again to hear the sounds from outside of her. The grass was full of hissing snakes. She gasped.

As if to find a means of escape, young Old Woman looked up towards the fruit trees. They were trying desperately to bud, adorned with draperies of limp snakes, and with entwining snakes constantly on the move. Here and there a red or pink belly showed through, almost cherry-blossom in colour. She had to make it to the upper end of the orchard; the pines and the thick bed of needles that lay under them, would be free of snakes. She must get there. But how?

The grass was growing snakes. The longer grasses, under the unkempt fruit trees, were being flattened by the mass of moving snakes. She knew not how she'd moved, walked, hovered through those grasses of snakes. But young Old Woman eventually stood under the massive limbs of the pines, with her nostrils full of the resin-rich air. Barely a snake ventured onto the bed of pine needles, and she could arm herself against them with fallen pine cones.

Like a fisherman's net, the chicken wire fence at the orchard's end was heavy with pine needles, blown grasses, and with fallen unopened pine cones looking like the scales of red-brown fish. The growth of the ancient pine roots had pushed the weathered grey fence posts to odd angles, and the wire netting was both taut in places or bulging loose, and full of dead needles and dry grasses. The wind's whistle through the pines drowned out the hisspering of the snakes. Then the needle bed rose, seethed, and bulged. It tore open and spewed out copper and chestnut-coloured thumb-thick snakes gilded in the patches of sunlight. Her body stiffened.

***

Old Woman sat bolt upright in bed. Sweat matted her hair to her neck and her nightie clung to her skin. Her palms were clammy and the softness behind her knees was wet and sticky. Old Woman's mouth was agape—a silent protracted scream pouring out. Her hands clenched and unclenched in terror. She swung her feet to the floor, and went for the shotgun.

***

Early the following week, Old Woman judged the first of the ripening fruit to be at its best. She picked and laid them, child-like, into her gathered-up apron. Some looked as if they were fly-struck, but she knew it was too early for that.

106

Peaches were her favourite. Their skin was a furry down, like that of a newborn pup. The flesh was rich, moist, and bright with the sun. Cool and refreshing as the moon. "Harvest Moon Fruit" she called them. Old Woman had planted the Harvest Moon Fruit trees, in that part of her orchard closest to her house. The position afforded them the maximum benefit of the sun, and her not inconsiderable protection from unwelcome peach fanciers and predators.

Old Woman was surprised, and cursed vividly at having to spit out shotgun pellets from her fruit. She thought about the pellets, long and deeply, and without resolution.

When she slept, it was with a dreamy peach of a full moon. Yet someone insisted on taking bites out of the moon. Then a rain of shotgun pellets fell from the sky, rat-a-tat-tatting on the roof and down the pipes into her outdoor bathtub. Then draining out of the tub's plug hole, becoming an endless water-python slithering across the droughted land as flood waters.

***

Old Woman awoke. Her arthritic fists clenched. She drew her knees up close, and awaited the snakes of dawn light, which might slither through her shutters and under her doors.

Slowly, in the dark silence, Old Woman began to recall a happier time in her past, and then that recollection unravelled into remembering the books in her childhood. There was a particular thick and black-covered history book, *Gods, Graves and . . .*, ah . . . oh! something? In that book was a picture Old Woman could never forget. It was a bare-breasted, yet regal woman, wearing a long layered, flounced skirt, with her arms stretched out and down. A priestess. In each hand, The Priestess held a thumb-thick slate-black snake.

Old Woman shivered, her skin goose pimply and clammy again. She felt the hairs stand up on the back of her neck. Her body shivered again. *You wouldn't catch me bare-breasted, not with snakes, nor at any other time.*

Old Woman sighed and her body softened a little. She sighed again. She'd made up her mind. In the morning, she was going into the orchard to cut away deadwood. There would be no snake hangers in her orchard.

Dancing with Dora

Janet Brenkman Williams

Wednesday afternoons were never the same after Dora arrived. For years, Wednesday had been the one day in the school curriculum that everyone dreaded. This is because when we lined up in the assembly hall, girls stared with trepidation at the line up of boys opposite them. Boys with grimy fingernails and smelling of mothballs (this was before the days of deodorant). And there was always Graham who possessed no handkerchief but found the sleeve of his blazer proved quite adequate for the job.

But that Wednesday was one no one was ever going to forget. That Wednesday all eyes turned as Dora entered the hall. Bust high, back as straight as a ruler, and as graceful as the figurehead on the prow of a ship in full sail. Dora was what my mother, back in those days, would have referred to as "buxom" and my dad as a "big lass". The glances that followed Dora's entry never faltered as she moved towards the line of girls against the wall. No one said a word, not even "Old Polly", also known as Miss Parrot—whose hand paused momentarily above the arm of the record player. Dora seemed completely unfazed by the sudden attention when she strode through the hall and took her place next to me. I froze as it seemed that the whole school was now including *me* in their gaze. 'Now,' Miss Parrot said. 'Take your partners and get ready for *The Paul Jones*.'

Thank goodness for that! I thought to myself. *At least we'll be changing partners as we go round and time with Graham will be mercifully short.*

But nothing started off as usual. There was a stampede as the boys left their side of the hall and moved towards the girls—chaos ensued with plenty of pushing and shoving to be the first to reach Dora. Miss Parrot shouted to no avail above the melee that ensued from the boys who had rushed across the hall. The music stopped, followed by a loud and long blow from a very noisy two-fingered whistle and Miss Parrot's infamous shriek for everyone to come to a standstill. 'Right. If you can't behave with some decorum then I will call out the boys' names and tell you who you will start dancing with this afternoon.'

Peace, to some extent, found its way over the rest of the session despite the trampled toes and ankles accidentally kicked. Except Dora. It didn't matter who she danced with, Dora's feet floated above the floor.

From that afternoon onwards, Dora was always the first to step forward and choose a partner. Each week she chose someone different and no boy ever objected when she took them firmly by the hand and waist.

***

When we returned to our classrooms that first Wednesday, for some reason I never quite understood, I was asked to move to the front and sit next to Dora. 'You can help the new girl settle in.'

And so, an almost lifelong friendship began. Although it made no difference to my popularity with the boys, which remained at zero. It did, however, start ongoing jokes from the older girls in Form 2C about my new "fat friend". Yet, Dora sailed through it all without any sign of hostility or hurt feelings. Those jealous of Dora's confident air labelled her arrogant but that was something Dora was not.

From that first day, I sensed something unusual in Dora's demeanour—a spark in her eye that hinted at a spirited soul with a passion for life. It seemed as if there was nothing Dora was incapable of doing and eventually, she became the most popular girl in our class— admired for the way she always seemed to bend any rules but come out unscathed.

I once asked Dora where she had learnt to dance so well but she just shrugged and said, 'I just enjoy it.' She was the best friend I ever had— funny, carefree, and loyal.

***

In those days, when I was growing up, the only way of keeping in touch with friends was if you had a telephone or used the phone box outside the local post office. But if your "Bestie" lived on the other side of town, or a long bus ride away, staying in touch was difficult.

In the beginning, summer holidays proved no obstacle for Dora and I. We met in town, went to the movies and shopped together. We even went to the local youth club together where, of course, Dora was a hit with her twisting and jiving. However, when we left school and looked for jobs elsewhere and eventually moved to bigger cities and foreign lands in search of more interesting lives—the threads of our earlier years began to fray and we lost touch.

***

It wasn't until many years later, when for want of trying to find some light entertainment amongst all the drama and dross on television, that I caught up with Dora again. Or rather, saw her again.

There Dora was on the screen in full colour, a glowing figure in scarlet satin performing with a gentleman of equal proportions under the name of The Dancing Divas. Dora looked great; still a big lady but still as light on her feet as she was when we were sixteen. Their tango was amazing to watch—timing perfect as clockwork.

I contacted the television channel but despite my explanations for the reason why I wanted to contact The Dancing Divas, my emails were left unanswered. When I finally got through on a landline, I was told that such information was not available to the public. I even took the train into the city and enquired at the grand reception desk of Channel 9DWA but was met with the same response. Realising I had to resort to more devious tactics, I returned to the city for the final program of *Stepping Out* and positioned myself outside the stage door. To no avail. The Dancing Divas never appeared.

Later, I learnt from the newspapers and the internet, that Dora and her partner had won the contest and been spirited off to a celebration gala at the Hyde Park Hotel. I tried to find Dora on Facebook and via Wikipedia but, once again, she disappeared from my life.

***

Life went on, as it does, through a few marriages and children who disappeared into adventures of their own. Despite the many invitations to visit or stay with the children it wasn't until my retirement years that I decided I needed to have one last adventure myself before it was too late.

So, I decided to visit my son Harry, who was now a successful real estate agent in the South of France. Unfortunately, I didn't arrive at his villa until late evening so I had no idea of my surroundings. But the pre-dinner drinks out on the patio and the post-dinner sunset made up for any disappointment I initially had about where and how Harry lived.

Following overdue hugs and reminiscences about childhood and family members, Harry was also eager to tell me of his latest interest in astronomy and far off galaxies. Despite my tiredness, Harry insisted we climb to the rooftop of the villa and look through his latest toy, which was the largest telescope outside an observatory I had ever seen.

The stars were wonderful. The satellites fascinating to watch as they danced across the sky. The moon was incredible when it came up as every crater and line stretched out—just a touch away from my curious fingers. I could have stayed much longer but bed beckoned and jetlag took me into a long and restful sleep.

The next morning, I woke to bright sunshine and silence. I walked out to the patio where I found a coffee pot, a large cup, croissants and a note on the table: *Got a very special client mum and can't afford to be late. Why don't you have a look around? Perhaps take a walk on the beach? Love Harry.* As I sat in the sunshine relishing my continental breakfast, I noticed there were several interesting islands and yachts further out to sea.

Up on the roof again, I managed to manoeuvre Harry's telescope and recklessly fiddled with knobs and levers in my attempt to refocus the lens but got startled by my son's sudden return. I froze in mid-sweep not just because the telescope began to tilt but because I found myself with a view of the beach below.

'Well,' I exclaimed. 'You didn't tell me about your neighbours, Harry!'

'You're in the South of France, Mum. There are nudist beaches everywhere but this one is open to everyone, naked or not. You can do what you want.'

'Well, I can see that,' I replied.

Harry laughed, tapped me on the shoulder and said, 'Come on, Mum. You said you wanted an adventure. Why not go down for a swim?'

It was true. I still had a reasonable figure and besides I didn't have to go completely bare. I could keep my pants on. *But did I dare?*

Two days later, feeling brave and ensuring the telescope had been realigned towards the heavens and not the beach, I ventured down to the bay with a large hat and an even larger pair of sunglasses. Comfortably dug into a hollow in the sand I started reading my latest paperback. My concentration was broken by the sound of a very English voice calling, 'Fresh English Cakes. Baked this morning.' I looked up and there was this mature woman with a Quality Street tin tucked under her arm striding confidently along the beach—completely naked. *There was only one person with a figure that great,* I thought. Even now after all these years.

'Dora,' I screamed.

She stopped in mid-step. I flung my sunglasses and hat into the air and ran towards her with open arms. Dora tossed the tin aside when she realised who I was. She grabbed me by the arms. We began dancing round and round and round as if we were the only ones on the beach.

Sink

Meghalee Bose

I'm tightening the lantern roped to the mast when the boat from behind knocks into ours again. The world lurches and my knees hit the wooden bottom. Brown water sloshes over the bow to puddle around my shins.

I grit my teeth through the pain and check on the tarp, which is slick on the outside and gleaming green in places under the harsh fluorescence of the battery lantern. The tarp is for ease of transport, not protection—I can see the shadow of Anisa's legs sticking out at the end. I pull the tarp a little snugger, tucking her in.

I lose some time stroking mindlessly over the rubber sheeting. The dinghy is stable when I look up again, barely rocking under our weight. *A little too stable.* I squint in the dark, surroundings murky despite the line of bobbing lights mounted on a queue of boats. The impact has angled us wrong, lodging the discoloured bow of the dinghy against an old streetlight.

Still wincing, I come up to my feet and pick my steps carefully to the front. From prow to stern the whole dinghy is less than three metres. The streetlight is rusty iron and algal green with a gaping empty socket where a lightbulb might've been a couple decades ago—a corpse of a thing.

Bracing a hand against the light pole, I try to heave the dinghy off. Mosquitoes dart frantically about my knuckles. The dinghy creaks and barely budges. I step over the tarp on my way to the back, its misshapen heap sliding with the shifting weight.

On the other end, the dinghy's stern is backed into the wall of a building. The number six is painted in stained white, just visible in the lantern's glow. I manage to secure a grip on a recessed window frame and push the dinghy straight.

Its prow bumps into the boat next to us and I ignore the litany of swears issued in my direction. We're crammed four to an avenue down here and have three blocks left to go. The water slips and slides, an odd tin can or rubber slipper or plastic bag spilling rubbish floating on by between the boats. The water is six storeys deep, evidently, even though the building before said seven. No one knows for sure, and it doesn't really matter. The floods are only getting worse.

I settle down at the bow, putting my hand out to the tarp. 'Calling them floods makes it sound seasonal,' Anisa said. We were both born with the city under water. The Garuda Sea Wall was already several metres below sea level. Where there wasn't water, there were potholes like widening cavities. Tsunami-felled coconut trees on abandoned roads. Leagues of cars left unsold and floating at second-hand dealerships.

Then, the elevators stopped coming down and the cross-building walkways swelled up with traffic. Anyone too poor to live more than ten storeys above got themselves a boat. It had gone past seasonal decades ago. There wasn't a patch of land to stand on, let alone bury someone in.

There's something icy-cold pressing against my ankle, where the tarp isn't quite long enough. There's no space to move away on the boat—like the nights Anisa and I spent back-to-back on the same bunk grumbling about cold feet.

I sit still and press into the insensate touch. Sisters making do.

The air is thick and my skin swaddled by the weight of its own sweat. Snippets of conversation drift over from the other boats. Some soft sobbing. Most of them are here for the same thing. Three boats down, where the floodway has narrowed to a couple metres with the obstructing mass of rubbish, three men in sweat-stained ganjis are playing a raucous game of cards. Municipal disposal in all likelihood. The funerals happen once or twice a month—we're all likely to be sitting here awhile.

I shiver. I've never liked being out on the floodways long, even if it was daylight. The low hanging fog dilutes the sunlight till it dapples the green, opaque water in ghostly imprints. Some patches of water light up like greasy, pallid rainbows. Some patches shine slickly while some are coated thick with ravenous algae. Sometimes when I dip a hand below the surface sludge, I can be misled into forgetting how many fingers are attached.

After all, water is darkness made real. I can flash a light into its depths and plumb nothing of what lurks below. What has sunk.

I continue to press into my sister's stiff heel. She was good at reassuring touches. Anisa would angle my chin upwards and point to a metre-wide pipe running down the length of a building and into the water. She'd talk about land subsidence and people from thirty, forty, fifty years ago pulling up groundwater. She'd talk about the illegal pumps in supermarkets, apartment buildings, and schools—pulling thousands of gallons till the ground sank and the water came to claim us anyway. Anisa's face would be aglow with the irony of it all. And by the end of the story, we'd be out of the floodways and back on solid concrete.

Sometimes, Anisa would picture the good parts: sandy beaches and ocean views of what was meant to be a paradise. 'It's not the same,' she'd say. For years, I watched my sister scrimp for old pamphlets and ripped textbook pages to put up on our shabby walls. 'It was blue.'

Still a vat of waste and dead things. 'It was *blue*,' she'd repeat. 'The colour didn't come from inside. It was reflecting back the world.'

The water is tar black tonight. My chest dammed up with something rotting.

We creep forward, hour-by-hour until the beachfront comes into view. It is a stretch of darkness uninterrupted by looming buildings. The line of boats continues on and breaks down into a disorderly cluster of lights at the far end. Out to sea, the undertaker conducts his business. Under the buzz of insect wings and people moving about their vessels—comes the occasional sound of a splash.

It's a lot of effort to deal with something mundane. Our father died before Anisa started teething. Back then, we rummaged for as many chains or tough plastic cabling we could find. Mother and a couple of her friends took Father, along with the trashed CRT TV which had been out by the hallway. They were back from the local flooded cricket pitch in a few hours.

Mother vanished before Anisa lost all her milk teeth. When it was her time, I imagine someone did the same for her. Found something heavy, tied strong knots.

Five or seven years ago, bodies started coming back up from the cricket pitch. All knots give way eventually to the buoyancy of death. The bottom was cold enough to slow the decay, which is why the bodies even stayed down that long. But you couldn't have half-rotted human limbs clogging up a perfectly useable thoroughfare. So, someone from up above came up with a viable solution to sell to everyone below. Now there's an undertaker with a hook-up operating at the beach. He pours a dribble into a jaw half-prised shut and the corpses stay sunk.

Still, no one cleared the cricket pitch and we all just moved away. Late nights, I think about my father amidst those gently floating figures in the muck with a set of perfectly preserved teeth.

It's dawn by the time we get close to the front of the line. I sit and watch the rippling black outlines of the boats in the lightening water. The people onboard get to work, chatting with the undertaker and heaving their cargo up to the front. The lingering smog seems to sever off heads, arms, and legs—odd silhouettes formed of their remaining parts.

The splashes sound louder from here. Motors kick up again and the boats turn around. A whistle blast echoes over the water and I blindly feel for the starting cord of the dinghy's bolted engine. One tug and we sputter forward, eventually bumping into the undertaker's stripped sailboat. The cord whips back from my palm, wet and slicing. The wait is over.

'That one?' I lift my head and dumbly stare up at the undertaker and his clipboard. He leans over the side, his weedy eyebrows scrunched in the direction of the tarp. 'How heavy?'

'I ... I don't.' Words finally skitter out, as I look down at Anisa. She is stretched out in the bottom of the dinghy and hidden behind rubber sheeting—playing at peekaboo. 'I'm not sure. She was ... nineteen?'

There's a scritch of pen over paper. 'You have payment?'

I have a sheaf of pre-counted notes in the pouch at my side. I lean up to pass them over.

The man wipes his palms before pinching the sheaf off. He pulls out a transparent little sachet, half-full of a white powder. He braces his hand on the side, like he's about to jump over onto the dinghy.

I stammer. 'Can I. Can ...'

The undertaker uncovers his teeth like a smile—incisors stained reddish with betel leaf. His eyes are unaffected. 'Easier if I do. Gets stiff.'

The dinghy tilts when he lands on the prow's edge. It's more weight than the little boat has ever had to bear. The man nimbly steps along the sides and stoops over to tug the end of the tarp loose.

Anisa's dark hair spills out, combed but lank. Her eyelids are the greyish white of mixed cement. The man seals one hand around her jaw and I whip my eyes away—staring down fixedly at the muddy green water like it's suddenly gone clear.

The dinghy pitches as the undertaker straightens up slowly. He's got two short ends of the tarp in his fists, staggering slightly under the weight.

His clipboard is shoved partway into the waistband of his trousers. Anisa's head lolls forward, unsupported.

We're at the front of the line. The thought pools up in my chest, lungs squeezing down around a cold weight I can't scream past. My legs quiver like they haven't in twenty years.

Maybe if we just … we could just go back. Start at the end of the queue and steal another day. Sail this avenue over and over, smog lingering over filmy waters, feet pressed close.

'You can do on your own?' The undertaker strains, adjusting his grip.

It's like there's water in my throat, lapping cold and agonising.

No. No, no, no.

But this isn't the time. It wasn't the time when the rusty scrape on her foot got infected or when the antibiotics were counterfeit. When she smiled, feverishly aglow, for the last time. When I kept the building up with all the wailing.

I'm letting her down.

The dinghy rolls under my feet even as I lift the tarp with all the gentleness I can manage. Anisa's sandals bump at the skin of my wrists. I think about her feet poking out of the water with her round toes half-submerged.

Then the undertaker pulls. Anisa lurches gracelessly through the air and splashes in. There is no struggle. No half-there-half-gone image to sear into memory. She goes straight through the water—green closing around her like a sinkhole.

I blink at the empty bottom of the dinghy where she once was. Then I look back again. There aren't even bubbles in the water. Just glutinous ripples fracturing from another boat's approach, waiting their turn.

My chest still feels throttled. There's no one else on the dinghy. The undertaker must have left. I drop down mutely, working on autopilot till the sputter of the motor shudders up my bones. The line is moving up. I'm drifting away.

I glance over my shoulder and the boats at the front are ten metres away now. Twenty. The sun has begun to pierce through the gloom in shafts—pale and shimmering. The soft sound of someone's cries begin to travel over the water.

I can't pinpoint the spot where I sunk my sister.

Carwyn

Steven Moriarty

Cherny falls for the fifth time. His head, against the forest floor, is comfortable. Maybe he should just let the woods take him. Moss him up. He stares at the towering Bunya Pines—their branches are raised heavenwards in welcome. Lunar grey clouds are hiding faraway suns. *Oh. Now it decides to rain.* A wet tap hitting one, two, then a billion leaves. *Lovely.*

Cherny had some romantic notion he could achieve target acquisition by tracking old school but between ideas and reality fall shadows, as always. Mists arise and darkness deepens. His old boots are getting wet. He's doubting his instinct. *Maybe sleep's the thing.*

Come on, Dad, up you get. His son's tender voice. That's what it takes to rouse him.

***

Cherny, you see, is a birder. Actually, a concreter by trade. Specialising in driveways on new, luckless estates built over mosquito-screaming floodplains. But birding was the childhood passion that endured. With cupped hands, Cherny had passed on this quiet pastime to his son. The concreting, well Cherny walked away from that. Birding had consumed him of late, soothing a mind that felt full of glass shards.

They were meant to do this trip together. The footage from his son's drone had left them both gobsmacked. Had they really captured the scarlet slash of the Ivory-billed Woodpecker? And the scruffy one that looked like it had just got out of bed. Could that really be a Philippine Eagle? On the encrypted birder site he used, someone anonymously and preposterously had sworn they'd seen a pair of Whooping Cranes. Someone else, a Californian Condor. But of course it couldn't be. This was the stuff of fantasy. These were all Grail birds. Why would some of the most endangered species in the world cross a hemisphere to winter here? Ridiculous. That was the consensus. Doctored images by despicable tricksters. Well, the others might have been. *Who knows what to believe nowadays?* But Cherny son's footage. That was tangible. And so, the question remained: Why? Why come here? Obviously, it had something to do with the alien incursions.

***

The canopy protected Cherny from most of the rain but still. With a sigh, he clambered upright and admitted that maybe his tracking wasn't so good. He reached into his pack for the goggles. And the goggles change everything.

That leaf. Infinitely recursive. The intricate reality of it overwhelms. Fractals reveal fractals. Is he falling? He dares look at the trunk of the nearest tree, bejewelled with beetles and unnameable, little things, snuggling, burrowing, talking in colours he never knew existed. Every little illumination, each now-you-see-me-now-you-don't photon. Cherny's hand writhes in ancient and snaking Celt patterning. It's all too much.

He breathes slow, deliberately calming himself. Reluctant to look up, just in case he is buried by this collapsing sense of self and place. The blindness of humanity. He hadn't known the real was like this. *Breathe, Cherny. Breathe.*

He gets a grip. Returns to himself. *Well done. Pat on the back.* Maybe though, it's not him. Maybe the alien tech has taken pity. He looks at his hand again. It's just his hand. The visuals have definitely scaled back. Finding himself relying on the kindness of mathematical transforms and compassionate recalibrations, a laugh escapes. He feels better. So, try again.

A forest floor of movement and colour. *Check. Okay.* He's got this. He looks up. He's in a magical, childhood dream done by Monet and edited by Warhol. The splendour now is tolerable. He reminds himself again to breathe. To be cautious. He could lose himself if he is not careful. Wake up in a hundred years.

Cherny's sense of direction returns. He sees now how the goggles reveal depth. The colour palette desaturates and cools with distance and is richer and warmer up close. *My god. What an amazing thing is life. And these goggles. Unearthly.*

***

The trade in weird tech was very hush hush around these parts. These parts being the old Mapleton Forest, part of the Blackall Ranges, the Sunshine Coast's hinterland contribution to the Great Dividing Range. All these dull words of Empire. In reality, this was Jinibara Country. And for the last decade or so, also a Bunnings car park for alien craft. Everyone local knew.

The State, well they told you nothing of course. A policy of enforced Silence. That hoary old tactic. Then, three years ago, a massive collision had lit the sky. They couldn't Silence that. Charred bones and alien bric-a-brac littered the land. A boon for opportunistic treasure hunters. Treasure hunters like Cherny's son.

The State responded by creating an Exclusion Zone round the whole of the Range. An impractical area to patrol. Not enough soldiers. Not enough working drones. Hadn't stopped anyone with serious intent. In acknowledgement of their shortcomings the State followed it up by legalising deadly force for trespass. After, Cherny had discovered his son's stash of alien contraband.

***

Cherny works his way slowly and patiently through the bracken. Sometimes following animal trails, sometimes creating his own. He walks at a gentle pace for an hour, on track, but also lost in the beauty of it all. Until he comes to the glade. And there, hovered the Shimmering. He backs up, stealth mode dominant. *So, it was true.*

Cherny hadn't believed him. He wished he had. Cherny wished for many things in relation to his son. Ahead lays an oscillating, blurry-edged circumference. Shrill rays of colour flare out, paining his temples. Back-lit giants trudge through. Creatures, monstrous to behold, arrange in groups and then efficiently disperse north, south, and west. Semi-transparent and glitching, even with his augmented vision. Legions.

Crouched and hidden, Cherny removes the goggles. And they are gone. He slips them back on and they're back. Invasion peak hour.

This was all a bit irritating for Cherny. *Go through hoops to get here being so careful with the patrols and now there's an alien army to deal with. If it's not one thing it's another.* But Cherny's a birder and he'll never, ever be anything else. *So, no sweat. Patience is a doddle.*

Cherny hunkers down. He digs into his pack, feels around, pulls out his flask and pours himself a cup of Oxo. The heat lifts his spirits. He nibbles a finger of Mr Kipling chocolate cake and watches the show.

Cherny's son had tried to tell him about these guys. Something about an inter-dimensional gate and an amassing spectral Cthulhuian army—whatever that meant. How they'd ignore you because the energy/reward ratio for complete dimensional transference just wasn't worth the effort. Not until sufficient forces at certain strategic locations had been reached. And so on. *Blah, blah conspiracy Twitter, blah.* Or so Cherny had thought at the time, only half-listening. His son's ideas had oft been outlandish.

The main point, anyway, was they were currently harmless—at least compared to the local militias and army types. Just in the way. *What else had his son said? Oh yeah, that's right.* How they weren't really monsters but omniscient multi-dimensional beings returning earthwards to harvest flesh crops which, news to Cherny, they had apparently sown millennia ago. But that had been his son. *Always banging on with the politics.*

Cherny sips his hot drink. Contemplates another finger cake. He likes these things and they do the trick on nights like this. *Can't have too many though. Far too sweet. And the packaging's ridiculous.*

***

An hour or so later, it's all over. Cherny gets up stiffly and has a stretch. Hoists his backpack and moves quietly as he approaches the portal. It gives off a tingle and smells of cloves. Even without the goggles on, the portal is compelling and hypnotic. He loses time and almost doesn't notice the birds. But he does notice them. Perched a few metres away are a pair of Ceyx melanurus as engrossed in the portal as he is. Cherny stands like stone. It's like seeing God. If God is two tiny kingfishers bedecked in metallic oranges and lilacs and blues. Preening and chattering they are. *They look happy.*

Cherny scrunches his eyes to clear the tears. He gasps as the clouds part and a fat full moon shines upon these little birds. Iridescence. *How could I be so blessed?* Yet, an immense longing for his son breaks him. *How could I be so cursed?* The birds hop and do more preening. Barely a hundred pairs back home in the Philippines. These fragile survivors. *Here. Well.*

Words are not enough. A flight of over five and a half thousand kilometres. *Why hadn't they stopped in Papua New Guinea? The forests are still strong there. What were they thinking? The Australian East Coast. These ranges. This forest.*

As if in answer, the Kingfishers rise. They fly right towards Cherny, diverting at the last moment—a shimmer of all the colours. Cherny follows their circles as they swerve through the trees. He sobs as the Kingfishers break the Silence with their song like squeaky, childhood toys. They dart towards the portal. They pass through. Out of this world. And now Cherny is alone.

After a while, in the crisp cold and stillness, Cherny thinks he's figured it out. The world is so hostile now. Somehow, the portal calls out to the few avian survivors. Somehow, they know there's a chance to evade the soul-destruction they've endured. *A chance to get the fuck out of Dodge.*

They'd named their son Carwyn. Cherny's love, Ceridwyn, dead these last twenty years, had been Welsh. Carwyn. Blessed One. Cherny wonders how the birds are doing. He takes a step. Then another. Then he's through.

Out of the Blue

Denise Kirby

Well, this was a turn up for the books.

He was still there and only a few feet away. Although, she could sense him more than see him. He was nothing more than a lump in the dark. How had she even got there? It had all been so rushed and confusing. She felt scrambled.

A sudden rough awakening. That was it. Yes, she had woken up and he was there. Demanding, almost shouting, dragging her out of the bed. Utterly confused, her mind had gone to that time, years ago, before Joe and the children. For a few seconds, she'd thought she was nineteen again and in that alleyway in Amsterdam. But then he'd yanked her towards the bedroom door and the pain in her troublesome shoulder had brought her back to her senses. Although, stepping barefoot through water had sent her a little off the rails again, making the whole thing feel like a dream.

She rubbed her eyes. Had she slept? How on earth she might have nodded off was beyond her. Half the time she couldn't sleep when she was in her own bed, let alone perched on a sloping roof clinging for dear life to a whirlybird. She wondered if the water would rise further and finish her off. She was wet through. Shivering. Or perhaps it was just her muscles twitching, unused to the effort.

The sky was lightening in the east. Very slowly, shapes were beginning to appear. Although not the ones she'd become accustomed to. Twenty-eight years in a house and you know every tree on the street.

They'd moved here after all the kids had gone. 'Something smaller to free up a bit of money and have some fun,' Joe had said, unexpectedly. Well, that hadn't lasted long. He'd reverted to character and exited just as the party was really kicking off—leaving her in the lurch with a trip to Europe all paid for.

How many years had it been since then? She should know. But she'd have to do the maths and, given the situation, she couldn't be buggered.

The full picture was being painted in, stroke after stroke, by the grey morning light. Water, muddy and brown, was up to the gutters. Up to the gunwales. Like a sinking ship.

Lucky she'd had her cataracts done a few years ago or she wouldn't be able to see more than a few inches in front of her nose. So, there was one way it could be worse, she supposed.

A cow floated slowly by.

Nextdoors were up on their roof too, huddled under the solar panels. The littlest one seemed to be in a swim ring, as if ready for a dip on a sunny day.

The father, Paul, waved and shouted something she couldn't make out. He tried again. 'You alright, Mrs Martinelli?'

She waved back. 'Yes, thank you,' she called but it came out like the voice of someone else. Weak and croaky. Old. Well, she was. How old exactly? She'd had trouble remembering her age for years. Not that she was doolally. She was always in the ballpark. But there didn't seem much point in remembering if you were eighty-two or eighty-three.

It was difficult to tell if the water was still rising. There was nothing beyond to measure it against. She wondered what they would do if it came above the roof line.

She could see the boy properly now. That's all he was really, no older than Melissa's youngest. What was Nathan? Fifteen? The boy was lying down, his feet against the roof edge, and seemed to be sleeping. Had his eyes shut at any rate.

She recognised his face. Yes, she'd seen him before. One of the boys that Moira Hannagan always complained about, the ones that hung around the entrance to the shopping centre. Jet black hair and almost red lips—a dangerous combination. T-shirt, shorts, and gumboots. He'd come prepared. She looked out at the vast water world. Although, not for this.

The question was … She realised this question had been sitting there the whole time just waiting to be asked like a wallflower at a dance. God, that brought back memories. *Wallflower. Honestly!* She was glad girls these days were making a fuss about how people spoke about them. No one called a boy a wallflower, did they? Not that she ever heard, anyway. The question was … how had the boy come to be in her house?

The water had risen quickly. In the time it had taken them to wade from her bed to the back door, the water had been up to her knees and he was yelling about the ladder. He'd left her then, hadn't he? Yes. She'd heard him sloshing his way to the shed, the light from his torch dancing on the water. These days, probably the light from a phone. She must have told him about it, the ladder, still on the side of the shed and hanging on the hooks Joe had put there when they'd first moved in.

By the time the boy had come back, balancing the uneven weight of the ladder over his head like a barbell, the water was up to her thighs. Greasy and cold. Full of unknown things that bumped against her and wrapped around her legs.

Then he was pushing her up. 'Go, go,' he was yelling as she faltered, fumbling on the rungs. When was the last time she'd climbed a ladder? Five years? Ten? When was the last time a boy's hands had been on her backside like that?

He wasn't with the emergency people. No fluoro vest. He hadn't knocked loudly on her door to warn her. No loud hailer strung across his chest. And, if there was one thing she was sure of—although, let's face it, nothing seemed set in stone at the moment. It could all just up and float away. The one thing she was sure of was that all the doors and windows had been locked.

Her life had been saved—there was no exaggeration in this and it ambushed her for a moment—her life had been saved by who? *A robber? Worse?* God had really had it in for her last night, even without the flood.

Everything in the house would be lost. The thought landed with a thud and she felt stupid that she hadn't come to it earlier. The drawings her father had done when he was just sixteen. Old videos of the children. The new mat in the back room. What a mess the green one was after Jasper had spent his last months there. Poor old thing couldn't always make it to the back door in time. She'd had to search high and low for a new mat with the right dimensions for her odd space. She wondered if the recliner chair would anchor it, stop it floating up, up, up like a magic carpet.

She imagined her lounge room then. As full as a fish tank. The book she'd been reading. Ornaments and faded photos. All the things of her life lifting gently off the shelves and swimming past. She felt untethered, as though gravity had lost its hold on her too. But again, her old body brought her back and she shifted her position. Her backside ached from the roof corrugations.

The boy sat up and saw the water cruelly sparkling in the sunrise. 'Shit.'

'Mm, probably. Mixed in with all the mud.'

He looked at her with astonishment. Then his full memory seemed to kick in and his face softened. Into what? Embarrassment? All that was irrelevant now. 'Thank you for getting me out of there.'

'Oh, yeah. I—'.

He jumped so easily to his feet and clambered up the roof a little way. For a better view. Or a worse one. *For better or worse. Now, there was a thing.*

The water level seemed to be holding steady. She supposed help would be along soon. Nextdoors would have called someone. They were both very good with mobile phones and whatnot. Or the boy might have.

Then what? Melissa's spare room with the sofa bed. Her back ached at the thought. Everything that was hers was gone. She was nothing but a bag of bones.

She followed the jagged form of a wrecked gazebo being carried along by the flood. She'd thought she'd experienced everything life could throw at her. That she could see how it would go on—her quiet days dripping away until it all drew to a close. You think you can't be surprised.

The boy slid back down the roof. 'Oh yeah,' he said, reaching into his pocket. 'I … rescued this too. Don't know why.'

Of all the things! A small tin from the kitchen with odds and ends in it that had been on the shelf for years. She couldn't remember the last time she'd opened it. Maybe he'd thought he'd find some cash.

Her fingers barely had the strength to prise the lid off. A lot of rubbish really: a tiny clay figure Melissa had made in primary school, some francs she'd bought in anticipation of that big trip (probably not even legal tender now), and a square wooden button. Underneath was a folded sheet of paper. Opening it, she shook her head, surprised she'd kept it. *To whom it may concern, Liliana (Lily) is a hard-working young woman, punctual and good-natured. She will be an asset to any company and I have no hesitation in recommending her for your consideration.*

She refolded the reference and tucked it back into the tin. A swarm of jet-skis suddenly ripped through the water and she was forced to rethink the comments she'd made about jet-ski owners to Moira last summer.

The boy shouted and waved. 'Jeff. Over here!' He turned to her. 'All you have to do is hold on,' he said, helping her to her feet.

Well, this was a turn up for the books.

Claim

Philip Enchelmaier

Two hundred dollars is not to be sniffed at. No matter how it comes to you. Especially these days. Pat had decided within a moment of peeling the Scratchie from the bus floor that it was hers to keep, even as its owner scampered down the aisle and disappeared unaware.

Thin bit of cardboard, yet the Scratchie stuck in Pat's pocket like a wrench all morning. She stared out across the empty dining room, pfftzed away the hair that had fallen loose as she bent down, plugged in, then straightened until her knees cracked. Pat's face was flushed from the effort. *Never any much mess to clean in Bistro Henri but still an effort.*

Headphones in, Pat let some Red Hot Chili Peppers drown out the silence and got on with vacuuming. A glint of morning sun shone in her eye. The silverware caught the morning sun even on dull days; or maybe it was still dazzling just from all the jewellery and gold-plated watches and shiny perfect smiling teeth of the previous night. She wished she could catch it too, whatever it was that people paid all that money for in a place like this—bottle it up, sell it, make a fortune, stake out her own little piece of the world. But all she could do was bus in, work and bus back home, an hour and ten each way. She bet no one who ate at Bistro Henri ever caught public transport. No one who ate here would think twice of dropping half a week's rent on a meal. No one who ate here was renting.

By the time she'd finished vacuuming, Pat had made a decision. *The Scratchie fell out of that woman's handbag. It was meant to be. Just as well!* The woman on the bus was a regular on that route. Pat didn't know her name, just knew that she smelt like booze and piss. *No offence.* The woman on the bus reminded Pat of her own mother, who she loved, but all the more reason. *Mum would've pissed it away, and that woman would've pissed it away, and who can afford to piss away two hundred dollars?*

***

One of the urinals was backed up. Plunger didn't work and Pat had to pour Drano. Something cruel was in the world, she'd known that for a long time. What Pat struggled to stomach was how cruelty always seemed to land back on her. All she'd done was work hard: roof over their heads, clothes on their backs, cleaner's wage at four shifts a week—five if she was lucky and picked up a Sunday.

Pat wanted to believe the universe was basically kind and good and all she had to do was put good into the world to get good things back. That's what Nikki said. Nikki would know. Nikki had done enough good to fit a size eight, marry up and out, and spend the rest of her life poolside in Phuket or wherever the hell she was now. Pat knew she can't have been as good of a person as Nikki … but she still must be a little bit good … done enough good for a two hundred dollar Scratchie.

The good she'd done had its moments. Mark couldn't sit still, Sarah always did her homework but always got it wrong, and Bec was sent home for punching a year eight girl in the chest and calling her a see-you-next-Tuesday. But Pat knew they were good at heart. They were hers.

Two hundred dollars. Two hundred demands. Two hundred dollars would buy new school shoes; buy a Christmas feast; buy a trip to the RSL club buffet; bottomless soft serve that Mark could barely believe was real. Pat knew her son dreamed of bottomless soft serve like she dreamed of home ownership and finding a decent bloody man for once and being free to just not panic all the time—like how she imagined the patrons of Bistro Henri must feel. She also knew that the kids would grow out of the shoes; get the runs from the buffet; Christmas meant fights over who had the kids for how long, why Lleyton spoiled them and was it just to show off, and who was that skank he was dating teaching Bec the c-word? Two hundred dollars couldn't stop that. *Can't raise them right on two hundred dollars. Can't raise them wrong without it.* What was the point of two hundred dollars? Two hundred dollars was a blip. Two hundred dollars was nothing.

All said and done, it wasn't like it was her wages. It was her reward.

***

129

Stepmother Jules only agreed to babysit because Pat had lied and said it was a date. Bec wanted a photo and wanted to know if her date had a job and how many people he'd murdered.

Pat was almost out the door when Mark broke the neck off Sarah's toy electric guitar. Sarah wailed and buried her head in Pat's hair, her hot tears streaking white lines through Pat's make-up. All the kids and even Jules thought Pat was going to the next suburb over to an oozy and overpriced pizza place. That was Pat's backup plan if courage failed. But she'd booked Bistro Henri, and she'd done her hair, and she'd done a casserole for the family, and now there was nothing else for it. At least she knew the way there.

***

The waiter welcomed Pat in a forced bright voice that was still somehow uptight. *Rude*, she thought. Not like the waiter at the pub, back when it was her local, before the divorce. Pat would joke and flirt and Lleyton would scowl and go quiet the rest of the night—peace at last. Pat still knew how to hold her own in a local pub. But Bistro Henri, in the evening …

It had been longer and harder to walk from the bus stop in heels. Pat felt flushed and sweaty long after she took her seat, alone at a table-for-two, and drank iced water from a glass worth more than her entire crockery set. *Everyone is looking at me. Judging.* The waiter left her to read the menu, retreating with a thin, knowing smile. *Dick. This was a mistake.*

***

Beef tartare with horseradish to start, spaghetti and spanner crab for mains, a side of charred leeks, and the crème caramel for dessert. Pat had planned her order with care and precision. From the two hundred she estimated thirty-odd dollars in change with which to shower gifts on her little terrors and lie about how she'd come into money.

The food reminded Pat too much of the food at her wedding and how she was supposed to feel so happy—so too-wonderfully happy. Her tongue was dry. She'd chewed too much gum on the bus over. Lleyton used to make fun of her gum. His own breath reeked of smokes and the meat pies and beer that left him too full for any of her cooking when he came home. Even his birthday dinner. Five hours prep in the bin.

The wine was lovely, she had to admit. She had pointed at something on a list written in French and hoped for the best. The waiter left the bottle on the table, but Pat limited herself to a glass. She was tempted to pour another, even just half a glass. But she thought of the thirty-odd dollars left over and the smiles thirty-odd dollars might bring to her beautiful monsters.

The crème caramel arrived and was gone in seconds. Now there was nothing but to stare out the window at the city below and check for messages from Jules and check the bus timetable and love-heart Nikki's latest post of her and her rich husband eating tapas in Madrid.

Then the bill came and Pat felt sick. Trapped under the spotlight under the waiter's fake sad self-righteous smile because he knew. He knew and he was happy that Pat only had two hundred, could only afford two hundred—but the bill was three hundred and twelve.

Gathering herself, Pat pointed out the problem with a shaky forefinger and trembling voice. 'The wine says one hundred and thirteen. Surely, the one at the front, an error? I only drank a glass.' Pat had been tempted to drink more, but she hadn't. She'd been good. Look, he could measure what was left. 'Thirteen dollars, surely? Not a hundred and thirteen?'

The waiter gestured calmly to the wine list. 'This particular wine,' he said, 'is only served by the bottle.'

Even though it meant public embarrassment, Pat cried and cursed and pleaded. It's not fair. It wasn't clear! 'How about writing a wine list in effing English?' she wailed.

Pat did what she could and it wasn't an act and it worked. They couldn't stand it and Pat knew that. A woman with a glimmering teardrop opal brooch beckoned the manager and whispered something. The manager whispered to the waiter. The waiter turned to Pat and smiled his judging bloody smile. 'Not to worry, the excess part of the bill is settled.'

***

Pat fished out change for a packet of vending machine crisps at the bus stop. Home again. Jules was asleep in the armchair and Bec and Sarah were in bed. Mark was up—the man of the house—always ready to defend them from robbers. Pat hugged him tight and told him that he definitely had to have a bath tomorrow. Mark asked about the restaurant and whether they had unlimited soft serve. Pat said, 'Of course, sweetheart.'

Undercurrent

Alison Davis

Yesterday, Dad took us fishing in the inlet. He showed us how to put the wriggling maggots on to our hooks and cast out into the shallow water. Mol refused to fish after Dad told her she'd have to wear a life-jacket. She chewed her bottom lip and glared at me and Jed as we mixed-up burley, using pollard and fish oil. Dad had brought the gear in a plastic bucket filled with tackle and hand-lines.

We tossed in the burley and oil pooled like a lily pad on the surface of the water. Mol pretended she wasn't interested but we all knew she was watching the tiny fish darting greedily towards the burley—sucking it in. We didn't catch anything, but Dad said fishing isn't about what you catch. It's about the wait. It's always about the wait.

Later, we played Scrabble on a picnic rug under gum trees. Mum cooked sausages on the barbie. Once it became dark, Jed and I lay on our backs and looked for constellations in the velvet sky. Mol fell asleep between us, cocooned in her sleeping bag like a caterpillar.

***

The clouds came in this morning. It looked like rain but Mum said there was no bloody way.

'Outside, the lot of you,' she barked. 'I don't need you three moping around underneath my feet.'

We hovered outside the cabin, scuffing our shoes in the soft dirt. Dad's face looked blurred through the grimy window as he washed the breakfast dishes—scrubbing at the scabs of Weet Bix.

I soared up into a star jump, stretching out my arms and legs as far as they could go. Dad was looking down at the sink and didn't see me. I wanted to go back in to ask Dad if he would take us fishing again … but it wasn't worth the risk. Mum would go mental if she saw me back inside.

'Race you to the tramp,' called Mol, picking up an old tennis ball. She tore down the dirt track towards the reception area. Jed and I gave Mol a head start, and then we set off too, easily overtaking Mol and reaching the trampoline first.

The tramp was a huge, spongey dome that rose out of the ground like a black rock—our own mini Uluru (this one was okay to climb). Dad said if we went to Uluru he would still try to climb it even though you're not supposed to. Mum said over her dead body.

The three of us jumped, getting higher with each bounce so that soon we could see the inlet. The water was dark and spiky plants guarded it like a line of soldiers.

'Let's go to the beach,' said Jed. 'There'll be huge waves.'

'I dunno. Dad said not to leave the campsite.'

Jed and Molly had already leapt off the tramp and started walking towards the road. I stood for a moment, wanting to stay, but already knowing that I'd follow.

***

I'd always been the cautious one. For my fourth birthday, Dad had built me a cubby house in the flame tree that grew in our backyard. He attached a rope ladder to one of its thick and horizontal branches so I could clamber up. I was too scared to climb the swaying ladder, but Jed, still in nappies, had shimmied up like a monkey. I sat silently while my parents laughed and cheered. Dad eventually built me wooden steps but by then Jed had claimed the cubby as his own.

The beach was deserted. Jed's footprints left a messy trail along the sand's smooth surface. He streaked ahead, lanky limbs too long for his body. Mol rolled in the sand until it caught in her eyebrows and eyelashes. We ran up into the sand dunes and slid down the slippery slopes. Jed found an old cardboard box and used it as a mat to give him extra speed. He flew past us with each round and screamed with laughter. We played games all afternoon.

'Throw the ball, Mol,' Jed called. He leapt up to catch it before rolling forward into a dive. He then threw it long and Mol ploughed down the sand towards the white froth. The ball was high and she ran with long strides, squealing as the water splattered up on to her pants.

'Jed,' Mol wailed. 'I'm telling Mum!' She grabbed the ball and hurled it up in a loopy arc. The wind caught it and pushed it back towards her. The ball floated in the air before sinking down with a splash, landing just out of her reach and floating in white water. The waves rolled in, collapsing in a whirl of foam and spray—snapping at the sand.

'I'll get it.' Jed leapt past us and waded out until the water came up to his waist. He stretched his arm, reaching for the ball. Then, a wall of water washed over him and propelled the ball into the air. We watched as Jed churned and spun like a limp T-shirt in a washing machine. At first, Mol and I laughed at the acrobatics. Then we were silent. I could see Jed was struggling to swim towards shore and the water was dragging him further and further out.

'Do not move, Mol. Sit here and do not move!'

Mol's face was fixed in a slightly crooked grin. I knew she was hoping that Jed was playing one of his practical jokes and any minute he would pop up, laughing, out of the swirling froth. I pulled off my jumper and tracky pants and waded in.

We'd grown up on the beach. Summers at Gracetown and winters at Rottnest, blue-lipped and slick in wetsuits. Mum and Dad had enrolled us in Nippers before we were old enough to protest, and soon the beach was part of our usual routine. But today, the ocean was neither friendly nor familiar.

The rip was just lines on the surface. Water bent and stretched. But I knew that below the surface the rip was rumbling, bubbling, and tugging. Jed was no match. He was suddenly a long way out, bobbing precariously like a bath toy.

I sliced through the water, kicking hard with my legs while feeling the weight of the water. The waves slapped at my face and pummelled my belly. I felt like I was going backwards but I pushed against the swell. Finally, I was close enough to call out to Jed.

'Swim across it!' The rip would be weaker now, far out from shore. 'Jed, swim towards me!' He seemed to be moving in slow motion, his thin arms hardly rising above the water. Stroke after stroke, Jed crawled towards me, until, finally, I was able to reach out and pull him in. We clung together, slippery as seals.

We swam beside each other, the water slapping at our faces. The ragged waves kept blocking our view of the beach but every few strokes we caught a glimpse of the white sand. We flapped and fluttered, slowly propelling ourselves forward.

For a moment, I was back in Nippers, proudly wearing my yellow cap that tied neatly under my chin. I could hear Dad's calm voice in my head: *Cut the water with your hands. Pull through it.*

'C'mon, Jed. We're nearly there.'

Gradually, the intensity of the water eased and a lighter blue signalled shallower water. I lowered my legs to feel the soft sand melt between my toes. Jed dragged himself from the surf and we collapsed, exhausted. Jed's hand brushed against mine, and it was as icy as a packet of frozen white bait.

'You okay?'

He nodded.

I tried to smile but my lips didn't move. I looked along the shoreline. To my left. To my right. The beach was pale with its emptiness.

And then, I heard a familiar squeal and saw flashes of colour high up in the dunes—figures scuttling across the sand like crabs. I made out Dad, running wildly at the front of the group. I raised my arm and he paused mid-stride for just a second. Dad had seen me. This time he had seen me.

Real Estate Agent Solves Byron Bay Rental Housing Crisis

Simone Schwarz

I haven't solved huge systemic social problems before. This is my first one but hopefully not my last. I'm not even that up to date with current affairs and news. But there are some things that it's hard to be unaware of. The latest celebrity to move to Byron. Which star was spotted with their children at the local playground. The age-defying beauty tips of insert any number of influencer names here.

No, seriously. Working in real estate at the rental end in Byron Bay and being a father of young adults—it's impossible to ignore the rental housing crisis. The crisis crept up slowly, over years, then went into overdrive during the pandemic. The Covid one that is.

More people left the city. More movies were being made in Australia, around Byron Bay in fact. They've even called the increasing real estate prices in Byron the "Hemsworth Effect".

Then the world became aware of Byron Bay. Would Byron Bay have the same attraction if it were named after one of the other New Romantic poets of Byron's era, such as Shelley or Keats? Perhaps. A rose by any other name, you know. It's not even named after the poet, but his grandfather, John Byron or "Foul-weather Jack". Now, I can't deny that Byron has had its share of foul weather. In 2020, the beach erosion was shocking. There are houses that are always at risk of being swallowed by a king tide. Not that that's impacted on real estate prices.

With the cashed-up mass arrivals seeking comfort and shelter, more owners tried their luck on the short-term holiday market. Yes, more homes taken off the long-term rental market and on to Airbnb. Or the luxury short term market such as with Byron Bliss Real Estate. Don't blame me for the name. I just work there.

Now, my daughter Kelly, and son Jack. Both twenty-something. Their friends are at that age of twenty-four out the door, as I told my kids growing up. Just to be clear about my expectations.

My girl Kelly said, 'You've made it crystal clear, Dad. You find somewhere that's habitable and not two-k a week and I'm out of here.' Then she headed out for a night of cheffing at one of the hatted organic restaurants in Byron. Glamorous as the restaurant is, the pay is drab and it's only the daytime lifestyle of surfing that keeps Kelly cooking. But before that she went, 'Oh, and Caitlin and Amy are coming to stay in the spare room. They are being evicted and the agent is raising the rent by five hundred a week. They've tried everywhere. You know what it's like.'

Me, I muttered back, 'This isn't a doss house. That spare room is meant to be my office for when I work from home.'

'You never work from home, Dad. You love the office gossip too much.'

It's true. On both counts. I had nothing on the books for the average person to rent and I never work from home. Still, I liked my home office. I took up decoupage during Covid. Unusual for a man. But I'm not hung up on gender stereotypes, as Kelly and Jack would say. I like to lay out my cut pictures and gold leaf. Brushes for varnish. Leave everything at the ready for when I can grab a spare half hour or two.

That won't be happening with more evictees in the house. It's a never-ending stream of people trying to find somewhere affordable to live up here. And it's getting worse. No comment on the gossip.

We've always attracted people who are homeless in Byron. Some prefer to live for free on prime real estate. Particularly in summer, on the beach or in the park—enjoying the multi-million-dollar views while travelling light. You know the ones, fire twirling and drumming. Young things that enjoy that lifestyle. But now there's a new level of homelessness. Older people. Women with kids. People with disabilities. Couch surfing. Sleeping in cars.

Then one day, I go into Bliss and it's the final straw when the owners of a solid, long-term rental tell me they've given their house a name: Byron Shack. Advise me that they want to list on the short-term holiday market. I told them, 'You do know the highest occupancy rates in Byron are in summer, specifically in the school holidays, right? We are going into winter, where the occupancy rates are between fifty and sixty percent, depending on the weather.' Everyone wants to be a housing speculator. There was no swaying them.

It was true I had about a third of the rentable properties in Byron on my books. Well, the computer, actually. For the next few months, many of the short-term rentals would stand empty. Beautiful homes, just sitting there locked up. Power and water connected. Clean, well maintained. No one in them.

Then I heard on the radio: 'A million empty homes in Australia on Census night.' I grabbed my phone and called Kelly. 'Kelly, tell Caitlin and Amy that the Byron Shack is free for the next month. I mean free, as in "empty" and "no cost". They just have to pay the cleaning fee at the end of the month. Tell them to come in and pick up the keys. Shit. Doesn't Amy clean the Shack anyway? Haha, she'll be able to pay herself.'

That was how it started.

I went on. 'What about that young nurse with the kid, I can't remember her name.'

Kelly said, 'Sam. Her little boy is Josh.'

'Yeah, are they still living on the couch at her Mum's? I'll text you the door code for Wave House. It's got ten bedrooms, so if you know any other families who need a roof, they might be able to share with her. But only for a month.'

'Dad, are you using your medicinal cannabis again? I don't know what you're up to but you're doing some awesome mid-life crisis stuff there. Love you.'

The movement of people. The balance of paid and unpaid short-term rentals required precision management. It was the equivalent of handling gold leaf with tweezers. Perfect. I loved it. My dexterity grew. My mind was sharper.

The software helps. Tenant tracking. Coordination of houses and bookings. Just these tenants are non-paying. Same process. The owners remain unenlightened. It's just the usual seasonal slump in rentals. I rotate the paying and non-paying clients. Every property owner just misses out on a couple of months of rent. Their houses would usually be empty for at least that period every year anyway. Optimisation of the housing stock.

Granted, it's not easy for people to move every month. But by about the third month, people have it down pat. Easier than couch surfing, especially when you're moving monthly from luxury to paradise. What more is there to say?

'Dad, what about finding somewhere for me and me mates?' Jack had cottoned on. He was leaning around the door frame of the spare room. I had tweezers in hand and was delicately picking up a small piece of gold leaf. 'What about Wave House?'

A guttural sound escaped my mouth as the gold leaf was pinched in two by the tweezers. Wave House is the ten-bedroom, ultra-modern compound right on Belongil Beach, owned by … no. I have ethics. I can't divulge who owns it. I also have morals, so I have no qualms about letting locals live in it. But maybe not my tradie son and his, choosing my words here, fun loving friends.

'I've got a few families in Wave House,' I spluttered. 'I'm only accommodating those in housing need. Those who can keep their mouths shut. Not those who want to brag about whose house they've been living in.'

'Jokes, Dad.' Laughs Jack. 'Just winding you up.'

'Ha. Ha. I'm doubled over laughing.'

'Guess what? Jonson Street wasn't gridlocked today and I managed to get a park without driving around for twenty minutes. And the burger place is opening for the whole week. They've got staff to cover shifts full time.'

'Wonders will never cease. Next, you'll be telling me that there are enough nurses and teachers.'

As you know, several other things are happening right now. Interest rates are going up. Inflation is biting. People are tightening belts and the first cuts are to discretionary spending. That means expensive weekends and holidays in, you guessed it, Byron Bay. People are assessing their options. Why go to Byron when you can go overseas for the same price? So, Byron Bay has a little less foot and car traffic and is a little less crowded, which has probably saved the town from its own popularity.

I have three hundred properties for rent in the system with a minimum of two bedrooms and the maximum is ten (you guessed it—Wave House). That's a hell of a lot of rooms to accommodate a lot of people. I am housing about six hundred people at any one time. Adults, kids, and families. With a resident population of just over six thousand, that's ten percent of the population, in case you need help with the maths. These are the kind of numbers that start to make an impact.

The shortages of workers are noticeably going down as those on low pay—hospitality, early childhood, NDIS, aged-care workers, cleaners, etcetera—can afford to live in Byron. They continue with their satisfying, but badly paid, jobs. They tell me they are saving money and building up reserves now that they aren't paying rent. Saving for deposits.

I know what you're thinking. When does it all fall into a heap? When does the A-lister turn up at the "unoccupied" Wave House to find Sam barbequing on the back deck while watching Josh and the other families happily swimming in the infinity pool. 'Oh, wow, this is awkward. Hi, I'm Sam. I'm a huge fan of yours. Sorry, we're just borrowing your house. We couldn't afford to rent anywhere. It's an amazing place. So beautiful.'

This happened. The mayor announced that the State Government endorsed a proposal to cap short term rental accommodation to sixty days a year in Byron Bay starting from September 2024. Two hours later, two A-list actors, one male, one female, you know them both, held a media conference.

'Thank you all for being here today.' A-lister said in her breathy voice. 'We have an important announcement that we would like to make public.' The media throng went wild. These two have never had their names romantically linked. It must be a new movie.

A-lister male spoke next. Rehearsed. Like at the Oscars. He was about to announce the winner. 'We would like to thank the Byron Bliss Real Estate Agents.' Complete confusion amongst the media throng. 'Who brought a serious situation to our attention. One which we feel we have the resources to do something about. We are giving our support to the short-term accommodation service: *Byron Bliss Clipped Stays*. This service is where holiday houses that are empty for a good portion of the time are offered to local workers experiencing housing needs.'

A-lister female continues. 'We act as ambassadors for many of the other owners who are also in agreement. People like us are so fortunate to be able to have houses in this magical place. We felt we should contribute. Give back. Smooth the social fabric of Byron Bay. Anyone who can afford a holiday home in Byron Bay and doesn't participate in this scheme—'.

It was male A-lister again. 'Is, in the famous words of an Australian Prime Minister, *a bum*.'

Good effort. We've got the Byron Bay housing crisis sorted. It gives me a breather to start working on my next projects. I'll be procuring more gold leaf. And I just heard about a local environmental issue …

Revelation

Stephanie Holm

On the night the red gum (which shaded the verge between 2 and 4 Corrigo Street) combusted, I was fifteen and drunk on Dad's homebrew because my neighbour Julie Robertson had broken up with me.

'The night's a blissful blur.' I'd heard my father use the phrase more than once in answer to Gina's (his second wife, my step mum, if you really want to know) probing questions after he returned from a night out. It's what I was hoping for ... but minds work in strange ways. I got neither bliss nor blur. I can still see the tree clearly: angry lava tongues of flame licking the sky, the panicked shadows, and a snap-crunch sound that makes my jaw tense even after the chasm of passing years.

The parts I wish I knew are clouded. Apparently, paramedics found me on the driveway, passed out. I came to with a freshly pumped stomach and a policewoman sitting beside my hospital bed asking questions.

Now, there is nothing left of the tree but a scarred stump that no amount of sweat or swearing has been able to shift. We were lucky, we were told, that the houses didn't catch alight. I didn't tell the policewoman (Angie, she wanted me to call her. Like we should be friends) that the occupants had been smouldering for weeks.

***

New people (the Donselaars) are moving into Number 2.

There was a removalist van parked outside yesterday, disgorging its contents. It's a regular occurrence, that removalist van. Nobody seems to stay long.

Minny Boo (she lived in Number 2 a few people back) said the place had bad energy. She was always walking from room-to-room burning sage. She painted all the walls green for healing.

The next owners, a young couple, said the green made them gag. They painted everything white. They didn't care what had happened. They said to me, 'We're not interested in ancient bloody history. Flipping it, that's where the money is. Bright white and light. That ugly stump has got to go too.'

I tried to warn the young couple that the present has its roots in the past and it wouldn't give them up easily. They didn't listen. The next thing, I heard the young woman shrieking. The whole street did, though it was the young man who was carted off in the ambulance. His thumb was apparently never the same.

***

The Donselaars are already at work in the yard, digging out Arum lilies. I watch them for a while. They stop by the stump and discuss something. Then he, Mr Donselaar, (I don't know his first name) returns with a chainsaw. *For god's sake. I better go warn them.*

'Hi,' I wave. The Donselaars look up and return the wave. 'You aren't trying to dig up that stump?' (The young couple plonked a letterbox on the stump in the end. They planted jasmine around it, but the jasmine climbed away from the dead wood, creeping up the fence instead.)

The Donselaars exchange a look. I can tell they think I'm interfering, but they invite me to sit on one of their still-packed boxes lining the front porch.

'So, what's the story?' Mr Donselaar nods towards the stump.

'The agent didn't tell you?'

The couple exchange another look.

'They said the house had a colourful history–but they assured us it had been renovated,' Mrs Donselaar volunteers. 'I asked if it was a meth lab.'

I laugh mirthlessly at the thought of Haman Robertson as a drug dealer. 'No, but he was evil enough.' I whisper to myself.

'Why? What happened?' Mrs Donselaar squeezes her husband's upper arm. 'I told you. I had a feeling.'

'Nonsense, houses don't carry the shadow of their prior inhabitant's sins. I was curious though…'. Mr Donselaar nods at the falling-down fence separating 2 and 4 and at the overgrown tangle of vegetation obscuring Number 4. You can barely see the house now.

'Does it have anything to do with next door? Does anybody live there?' Mrs Donselaar says and moves closer to her husband for comfort, or perhaps, protection. From this angle the place looks unloved, like nobody lives there. It's my ruse.

'You've heard the old witch rumour already then.' I say, nodding slowly. 'They keep themselves to themselves. It's not a meth lab.' A cackle escapes my lips. I press them together. The skin around my lips puckers. I turn back to face the stump. 'The tree caught on fire. A girl died.'

Mrs Donselaar gasps. She covers her mouth with her hands. 'How awful.'

'Kids playing with matches?' Mr Donselaar ventures.

The three of us eye the scarred wood. I can see the ghost of the tree with its thick limbs spreading, and the treehouse we'd built with timber from Dad's shed. You couldn't see the treehouse from the ground. It was secret, and safe.

'No, they knew better than to play with matches in a tree,' I say.

Julie and I had tiny lights—the type you attached to a keychain, bright enough to give a little light but not bright enough to draw attention. We used to say we were sleeping over at each other's house. Our parents weren't speaking by then, so there was no chance they'd phone up to check our stories.

Julie's parents were prim, priggish, and Pentecostal. Julie's mother moved through life like a ghost, silently and soullessly bending to her husband's will. That was one of the many things that gave my mum the shits. 'Why do they listen to him? That woman needs to grow a backbone,' she said to me one evening. The following morning, I woke to find she'd gone. Mum that was. She went to Africa, where the children needed her more than I did, apparently.

Julie's father, Haman Robertson, thought of himself as God's messenger on earth. He was no shining light. He swore and he smoked. I'd seen him standing by the sedge over the back fence—a cigarette twitching between his fingers after Julie dared to defy him. He was working on her soul too.

'Was it lightning? I saw a tree struck by lightning once. The whole thing exploded in flames,' Mr Donselaar says.

'Don't, Jack,' Mrs Donselaar says through her fingers, as though she can't bear to hear any more. As though it will poison the pleasure of their new home. 'So, which house do you live in?'

I wave vaguely at the road. 'Speaking of. I should be getting home.'

The deepening indigo of evening wraps itself around me as I leave the Donselaars, satisfied they won't try any nonsense with the chainsaw. At least not tonight.

I walk down the road and stop behind a weeping grevillea until the couple go inside. A light switches on in the front room. Mrs Donselaar's face appears briefly at the window before the curtain is drawn. Only then do I turn around.

The garden at Number 4 might look wild, but there is a hidden path to the back door. I let myself in. The shadows creep across the room and fill the aged kitchen. I stop at the bench and look out the window. Memories overtake me.

I see Julie and me as fifteen-year-olds hovering in the shadows beside Dad's shed (before the wisteria choked it).

The moon is full, like it was that fateful night. We are talking. It is the last time we'll speak, but neither of us knew that then. I was only focused on me, on how her words made my insides writhe.

'Dad knows,' teenage Julie's eyes glow with fear. 'He knows about us.'

'He can't do anything about it.' My ghost is full of youthful naivety. 'Don't worry about it. We can still meet secretly.' I watch myself offer Julie a drink. 'Dad won't notice one beer missing. He's got enough on his plate keeping Gina happy.'

Julie laughs but her body is tense. 'I wish your father was mine.' Then a shudder ripples through her. Teenage me tries to hug Julie but she pushes me away. 'No, I have to go. He's scarymad.'

A light flicker in the window that used to be Julia's bedroom. The two ghostly girls in the yard vanish, though they linger inside my head.

Inside Julie's old room, a figure prowls. My heart stutters and my fingers pinch the bench. The figure is not Julie's father. It is Mrs Donselaar sifting through boxes.

'Was it a crime?' Mrs Donselaar had asked me that afternoon as I'd turned to leave. In Haman's eyes, Julie's and my love was. 'The cause of the fire?' Mrs Donselaar pressed, her voice desperate for a denial.

'It was a cigarette,' I had said, finally. *But Julie didn't smoke.*

Gondwanaland

Courtney Collins

Mary wants to tell Father Bubu Singh that, like him, she did not arrive here with nothing. She came from Ireland, and he came from India, so they have leaving their homeland in common. But the fading light and whiskey are loosening so many things in Mary's head and as they sit in the glass room overlooking the rectory garden, she says, 'Father, how does a person heal?'

In person, Mary calls him "Father", but Bubu Singh is a young man really—even younger than her son. In her private thoughts she calls him Bubu Singh. He is someone she has come to love for the kind, deep way he listens and the surprising things he says.

That afternoon, when Mary finished vacuuming the wide rooms of the rectory, Bubu Singh invited her to join him for a drink, as he always did. In the glass room, they have already talked of Gondwanaland—a long ago time when India and Australia were joined in a great landmass before tectonic movements caused them to drift apart. As Bubu Singh described it, eyes wide, arms sweeping in front of him, he reminded Mary of her late husband. When he was young, this was how he spoke—believing all things were connected and we were all part of something bigger even if we didn't always feel it.

As Bubu Singh sits back in his armchair, Mary now wonders if he heard her question or if she even said it aloud. There is a long silence which she interrupts with the news she has been holding onto.

'My son is coming for Christmas,' she says.

'Only twenty-one days away,' says Bubu Singh.

'He's bringing his wife and my grandson with him. You know I've never met them.'

'Where will they stay?'

'With me, Father. With me.'

Mary lives in Brentwood Street, one of the oldest streets in the town. She has had the means to keep her house in good shape and her garden tended and tidy. But next to her is a house that has never been loved, not in all the decades Mary has lived there, and not with any of its changing owners.

'Perhaps he could buy the house next door and fix it up?' says Bubu Singh.

'He's a DJ,' says Mary. 'I've no idea how much money he makes.' It has taken Mary some time to convince herself that being a DJ in Bangkok is even a job.

Bubu Singh rises from his chair and collects Mary's empty glass. She is relieved he is pouring them another drink, even though they usually stop at one. She would like to flip up the footrest, recline, hear more about "Gondwanaland". But when Bubu Singh sits back down, he looks serious, overcome. He leans right into his legs, bows his head, holds the glass of whiskey with both hands like he is making an offering.

'Mary,' he finally says. 'What is time calling you to do?' She feels her mouth fall open. It does not sound to Mary like a Catholic question or anything Bubu Singh would have learned in the seminary. 'What is time calling you to do?'

'I heard you, Father.'

Mary stares at the carpet she has just cleaned. Something is glinting, tangled in its fibres. Mary's mind whirs and she lands on one time in particular. She was nineteen, working at the telephone exchange behind the post office. It was the tone of the young woman's voice and the knowledge of who the young woman was speaking to—a priest. Mary could not get off the line. She listened to their whole conversation. Later, on a break in the tearoom, two girls, her friends, told Mary she looked pale. Mary confessed.

'We've all done it,' the girls said. 'We all listen in from time to time.'

So, Mary repeated what she heard the young woman say to the priest and what the priest said to the young woman. Then she took in her friends' gasps and sympathies as if they were meant for herself.

***

147

'What is time calling you to do, Mary?'

Usually, Mary loves to listen to Bubu Singh. The sound of his voice and the way his soft words unfurl inside her. But this question keeps landing her in places she doesn't want to be.

It was 1986. The year of Halley's Comet. The year her husband dropped dead. They'd been married nine years. Their son had just turned eight. She had left her husband and son in the backyard—searching for the comet with their binoculars. When she returned with bowls of ice-cream, her husband was lying face first on the grass and their son was on top of him, trying to roll him over.

Mary springs out of her seat. 'Time,' she says, 'is calling me to go home and make the dinner.'

***

Walking up her steep hill, Mary remembers that when her husband died her brother came over from Ireland to help her. But he was no help. The first thing he said was, 'Bad luck comes in threes.'

'Why would you ever say that?' she said.

'It is just a saying,' he said. 'It is just what people say.'

'Heartless people,' said Mary. 'Stupid people.' She wanted to wipe her brother's words away.

Only days later, Mary's brother was walking back from the greasy spoon when he fell and broke his leg. Then Mary had to look after him and she could hardly look after herself or her son. All her brother ate was sausages and bacon and soon he was too fat for crutches.

Unlocking the front door of her house, Mary forgets her brother as her son comes to mind. She clocks the fact she hasn't seen him in fourteen years. What has she been doing all this time? Sitting at the café in Bridge Street, slurping on cappuccinos with her girlfriends, ordering soy milk or oat milk and learning about these new allergies. A welcome change from their previous conversations. For years, all they talked about were priests who were being sent to prison.

Inside the house, Mary does not prepare the dinner but begins again to clean. She vacuums and thinks of how much glitter was in the carpet that year of Halley's Comet—back when so many of her son's school projects required it. Wasn't she still vacuuming it up years later? And wasn't there a time she wasn't vacuuming at all?

After her husband dropped dead at thirty-five, Mary felt the only time she wasn't dying herself was when there was no one else in the house. She craved being alone. Finally, when her brother returned to Ireland, the local priest and nuns swept in—offering their kindness and offering to take her son on one camp or another.

It was about twelve years ago when Mary and her girlfriends started speaking about it. This was back when they gathered at the café after mass. There would be a Royal Commission. So, they couldn't avoid it. And it was at the café Mary learnt one of the priests accused was the same priest who took her son on those camps.

'I will never step foot in another church again,' Mary said.

'But it's the peoples' church,' one of her girlfriend's said. 'They can't take that from us.'

But they had already taken so much. Her son was living in Thailand then. Mary wanted to have the conversation with him face to face but when she suggested she visit him, he said it didn't suit.

In the end, Mary told her son about the priest on the phone and even with so much distance between them, when he fell silent, she knew what had happened. She felt it in her bones. But how was it she had not felt it before?

Mary pushes the nozzle of the vacuum cleaner sharply into a corner. She stops to shift the lounge. She imagines a Christmas tree, presents and a gingerbread house like the one in the window of the bakery. She imagines inviting her grandson to smash the gingerbread house with his little fist. She imagines cheering him on as he smashes it to pieces.

***

Each year on Christmas night, for so many years, Mary's girlfriends (the ones who are left) get together. They take turns sitting in each other's backyards under some arrangement of coloured lights with prawns sizzling on the BBQ as they drink Cinzano and soda with big chunks of ice. Mary and her girlfriends call themselves Christmas orphans because their children all live so far away. They exchange small gifts. Found or handmade is the rule and Mary has so many lavender eye masks now she could sew them together and keep the draft from under her door.

For the past five years, Father Bubu Singh has been their special guest. They are usually drunk when he arrives at 6 pm. Coloured lights swinging over his head, each year, Mary watches the way he balances his plate on his long legs and eats so elegantly—always lending an atmosphere of something holy even to an unholy place. And every year, Mary thinks: *At least there's one good one.*

***

Mary strips the sheets from the spare bed and remembers herself at seventeen. Pregnant and alone in her mother and father's house who had both passed, she was sprawled across their bed, worrying about what to do next. She knew what happened to girls like her who stayed. That night, she woke to her old dad standing at the end of the bed pointing to the mattress. She sat up and said, 'Dad, you're dead!' And then he vanished in front of her.

In the morning, she examined the mattress, running her hands over its lumps and patterns of flowers. She tipped it off its springs, leant it against the wall. And there, sewn into the underside of the mattress, was a perfect handstitched square. She snipped at the stiches and stuck her fingers inside. She felt notes tight rolled with rubber bands. She prized the rolls out and counted three thousand pounds. 'Thank you, Da. Thank you,' she said, looking up to the ceiling.

The next day, Mary booked a flight to Australia—the most faraway place she could think of. She had enough money to live on until she found a job and enough money to pay for an abortion when she got there.

***

This year, on Christmas night, Mary will not be sitting in any of her girlfriends' backyards—not even for the love of Bubu Singh. She will be at home with her grandson listening out for the truck that rolls down her street and for a man dressed as Santa ringing a bell and throwing out bags of sweets.

In the meantime, she will clean and press everything—even the sheets. When her son, his wife, and her grandson arrive after their long flight and train ride, everything about the house will say: "Welcome". They will meet no resistance, not even a crease.

Smoke and Berries

Louana Sutcliffe

The cemetery sat on the north-west fringe of town. The town was old, so the cemetery was huge, with rows of gravestones marching orderly across the grounds. Some stones were short and squat and uniform like pawns, others were towering like bishops. I'd only been to the cemetery twice before, both visits only during the day, like a normal person.

Beth wasn't a normal person. She wore black skivvies under her school shirts and layers of chunky crystals hung from worn leather cords around her pale neck. Beth spent most of every class doodling in her books, except art, which she spent doodling on a canvas. Beth seemed to exist on her own planet and seemed to like it that way. When I'd asked if Beth wanted to hang out that weekend, I hadn't really expected her to say yes. I also half-thought she was joking when she suggested the cemetery on Saturday night. I'd nearly backed out, but Beth was cute in the way jumping spiders are cute. Plus, she laughed at my jokes in English.

Tom had said I was crazy. I wondered if he was right as I pedalled my bike through the dead streets toward my date. The wrought iron archwayed entrance was flanked by two ornate light posts, one of which had blown out. As I got close, I saw Beth leaning against one of the posts. Beth stared out past the gravestones and only acknowledged my existence when I pulled up next to her.

'Hey,' I said.

Beth gave me a flat look and pulled at earphone cords I hadn't noticed until then. The earphones flopped over the collar of her shirt. 'What did you say?'

'I said hey.'

'Oh. Hey.' Beth shoved her hands into the cavernous pockets of her cargo pants.

I picked at the rubber on my bike handlebars. 'What're you listening to?'

'Marilyn Manson. Do you like him?'

'Um, yeah I guess.' I'd never heard the guy but all the pictures I'd seen with his weird eyes and metal teeth convinced me Beth was definitely on another planet.

Beth didn't look convinced. 'C'mon,' she said before walking through the archway. I rolled my bike along beside her.

Cloud had blown in late that afternoon. As we got further from the lone light post, the inky night swallowed us up. Beth weaved through the gravestones and deeper into the cemetery. I did my best not to clip any gravestones with my bike. My skin prickled, but I told myself it was just the autumn breeze creeping down the back of my collar and not the fact that I was walking through a maze of graves.

'Do you know where you're going?'

The dark shape of Beth's head turned. 'Yes.'

'Good, 'cos I can't see shit.'

'That's the point.'

I laughed. 'If it's gonna be like that, my mum's not home.'

'It's not like that.'

Ouch.

'Here.' Beth stopped and I nearly slammed into her. The gravestones loomed over us like old dead trees, making the night feel closer and darker. Beth sat down. I went to lean my bike against one of the gravestones, thought better of it and laid it down behind me. I joined Beth on the grass.

Soon, the cloth of Beth's pants rustled and then click—the bright glow of a lighter illuminated her face. Beth passed the cigarette to me and I tried to act like I'd smoked before, balancing it between my fingers the way mum and her wino friends did. A sweet brush of something berry-like crossed my lips—Beth's lip gloss, the taste of her lips—before acrid smoke swirled into my nose and down my throat.

I coughed and inhaled more smoke. I coughed again. Then I passed the cigarette back to Beth. She laughed and took a long drag, the orange glow of the cigarette swelling then fading. I was thankful it was dark.

'Is this like, a regular Saturday night for you? Smoking in the cemetery?'

'Yeah, I come here heaps.' Swell. Fade. 'Usually alone, though.'

I felt her eyes on me. Beth's words lingered between us expectantly. Then she scooped her knees to her chest in one fluid and cagey movement.

She turned her face away again. The cigarette disappeared as she took another drag. I wondered what I'd said …

Beth finished her cigarette and rolled the butt under her shoe.

'How do you get past your parents? My mum would freak if she knew I was here.'

The outline of Beth's shoulders shifted. 'They don't care.'

Man, she is making this hard.

'My mum's a nurse. She's on nights this week, so she won't be home until tomorrow. Got the house to myself.'

'Where's your dad?'

'In Sydney or something, I don't know. I never see him.'

'Must be nice.' I could hear Beth plucking at the grass.

I changed course. 'I really like your art.'

'Oh. Thanks.' The smile in her voice was cute.

'I wish I could draw but I really suck at it.'

She giggled. 'You don't suck.'

'You're a terrible liar.'

She laughed and stretched out, leaning back on her elbows. Her face lifted toward the clouds.

'Did you want to go back to mine? It's not far and I've got some pizza left over. We could watch a movie or play the PlayStation?'

'Nah.'

This is why she doesn't have any friends, I could hear Tom say. I mimicked Beth's position. 'What do you want to do, then?'

'Wait.'

'For what?'

'Just wait.'

I flopped fully onto the grass and linked my fingers behind my head. *For what?* A few stars had broken through the clouds and their sparse twinkling amidst the sea of black struck me with a weird loneliness. I untangled my hands and reached for one of Beth's. She jerked away and sat up.

Damn. 'Sorry, I didn't mean—'

'It's alright.'

She stayed hunched forward and I re-linked my hands. I stared at the stars. There were more now. I wondered what Beth was thinking about but I was too afraid to ask.

The sky opened as the clouds drifted apart, revealing a full and creamy yellow moon. Low, rich, and swollen, the moon gleamed across the gravestones. I sat up and a glow spread across our laps. Beth's head was turned toward the tallest gravestone near us, just to her left, and I followed her smile. The strange glow increased to the top of the stone monolith. The pinnacle shone with a cool, bright light that radiated across the nearest rows of gravestones.

'Whoa.'

Beth beamed at me. Her pale face was soft in the light. Her bright eyes flicked between mine, searching again.

'Do you like it?'

I finally understood.

'Yeah, it's awesome. How's it glowing?'

Beth looked back at the gravestone. 'I don't know. There's a glass box on the top but I'm too short to see inside. I don't want to know, though. It's better this way.'

'Mysterious.'

She half-smiled. 'Yeah.'

'Thanks for showing me this.'

'Thanks for coming. I know it's a weird idea for a date but it's really cool.'

'You're really cool.'

She laughed again. '*You're* a terrible liar.'

'Nah. I think you're cool, Beth. Different cool.'

The night wasn't dark enough now to hide the faint colour in Beth's cheeks. She looked out past the gravestones. I wanted to reach for her hand again.

'Do you want to listen to some music?'

'Yeah.'

She slipped the earphones out from under her shirt and passed me one side. I had to shuffle close for it to reach. Beth laid down and I did the same. Shoulder-to-shoulder we watched the sky.

The music started. Haunting synths and whispers about space and the stars filled the silence between us.

'What are we listening to?'

'I knew you hadn't heard Marilyn Manson.'

'Heh, whoops.'

My hand slid from where it rested on my stomach and brushed Beth's. I pulled away reflexively but her fingers closed around mine, soft and delicate, and held me there. And there I stayed.